HAYLEY M. MOON

Bloody Endings

Book 2 of the Coven Origins Series

BLACK MELANCHOLY

Cover design: Covers by Nain via Fiverr

For information regarding permission to reproduce selections from this book, contact the author via www.hayleymoon.com.

First edition

ISBN: 979-8-9989753-0-1

This book was professionally typeset on Reedsy.
Find out more at reedsy.com

For Darlene and Mary.

Contents

1

Amending Plans

Caesar snarled, slamming his palm against the table. The resounding crack echoed through the chamber, sending ripples through the glasses set before the council members. They kept delaying the Rite of Selene, and with it, his rightful claim to the mantle of Alpha—the power he was born to wield.

Elijah sighed, swirling the amber liquid in his glass before rising to his feet. His gaze met Caesar's with the weariness of a man who had seen this battle waged before.

"I understand your frustration, but it's not that simple," he stated, measured and deliberate.

"Before his unfortunate and untimely death, your father named your brother Alpha. He did so before many of the coven. That isn't something we can ignore."

Charles remained silent, his hands folded in his lap as he observed the impromptu gathering. Tension coiled around the room, thick as a brewing storm. Voices rose, some in favor of denying Caesar the title he had spent a lifetime reaching for. Others hesitated, glancing between each other the weight of uncertainty on their shoulders. Maximillian had told him enough before politics had driven them apart—his late friend's youngest son was not one to be underestimated.

Neil leaned forward, his sharp gaze sweeping over the assembled council.

"Is there a problem with allowing him," he gestured toward the head of the table, "to proceed with the ceremony?" His tone was casual, but there was an edge beneath it. "Armand is missing. Maximillian is dead, and unless I'm mistaken, the boy is the last male descendant of the DuBois clan. I see no reason not to carry out the Rite of Selene." He leaned back, nodding as if the matter were already settled.

Across the table, Reynolds' gaze darkened. He opposed Caesar's ascension just as much as he opposed this so-called Federation but now was not the time to speak. Frank was still missing. Neither his wife, his staff, nor the young woman he frequented had seen him in over two weeks. And yet, the interim Alpha had not sent a single scout to search for the senior councilman. That, more than anything, made Reynolds uneasy. Opposition was being eliminated.

"You expect to take over in the middle of this chaos?" Charles' voice cut through the chamber, each word weighted with the unspoken fears of those around him. "News of Maximillian's death has spread far and wide. People have lost faith in the American Coven. A councilman is missing, and no scouts have been deployed. And yet... you expect us to move forward with a crowning ceremony?"

He spoke what many only dared to whisper in private, their silence rooted in fear.

Caesar's eyes darkened.

"Watch your words—and your tone," he warned, voice smooth but laced with steel. "Don't mistake your friendship with my late father as leverage."

The tension thickened. Caesar continued staring Charles down, his grip tightening at his sides. The fine fabric of his sleeves did little to stop the hairs on his arms from rising. He had anticipated resistance after his father's death, but not this level of outright defiance. The High Table and the Council weren't just hesitating—they were rallying against him.

Then there was Charles... he hadn't accounted for Charles.

He had dismissed the man as a lackey, a spineless figure content to play the role of an obedient follower. But now, standing before him, Charles held the room in a way Caesar hadn't foreseen. If the doctor refused to move forward, the others would fall in line behind him. Just as Frank had warned—before Caesar fed him into a woodchipper.

Charles bristled. If this was a challenge, he would gladly accept. His gaze flickered to the two men who had stepped forward. They were new. No doubt, Caesar's hired muscle. If they had come through the proper channels, he would have known them.

Not here. Not now.

Fighting one? Maybe. Two? Possible. Three plus Caesar? He wouldn't get the chance to complete the shift before they were on him.

He exhaled slowly, letting his shoulders loosen—a calculated display of ease. This temporary stand-down was nothing more than a performance, a move to lull the interim alpha into complacency and hopefully buy Charles more time.

A chair scraped against wood, the sharp sound cutting through the tension. Charles's hand twitched, instinct bristling beneath his skin. A moment later, a weighted hand settled on his shoulder.

"We're all concerned," Reynolds said smoothly, his grip firm before he let go. "This new Federation. The whereabouts of your brother. And I'm sure Charles here is worried about his daughter. Like any father, he wants her home."

Reynolds stepped around him, his presence deliberate. His gaze met Charles's, and for a split second, his eyebrows flicked up—a silent message. He turned his attention to Caesar. A few men murmured, shifting uneasily.

Charles had no more moves left. If he wanted to stay off Caesar's hit list, he had to play along. He had to make it look like he accepted this so-called Federation, like he recognized their new alpha's authority.

"I apologise," he said, his voice measured. "I'm still in shock over your father's death. He was a longtime friend. You remember, we grew up together…" Charles let a momentary somberness cloud his expression, just enough to sell the lie.

It worked. Caesar's posture eased, the rigid lines in his face softening. Across the room, two men shifted. The nod Caesar gave them was slight, but not unnoticed. Silently, they stepped back into position.

Caesar flicked a hand through the air, dismissing the conversation as if swatting away a fly. He had no patience for dramatics. As far as he was concerned, the old ways were dead.

"Yes, I'm aware," he said, voice smooth but edged with finality. "But the past is just that—the past. We all feel the loss of our alpha. My sister and I more than anyone. Especially since it was our brother's doing."

Charles gave a slow nod and lowered himself into his chair. Across the room, Reynolds hobbled to an empty seat, settling in with a measured sigh. His expression remained unreadable, his sharp gaze moving between the men gathered.

"I'd suggest we table this conversation until after your wedding reception," Reynolds said, straightening his tie with deliberate ease.

Caesar exhaled sharply. "Fine. But we resume tomorrow."

"Tomorrow?" Reynolds let out a quiet chuckle. "Your honeymoon? Surely, that's not something you'd like to miss."

Caesar's jaw tightened, his fingers curling against his palm.

"Postponed. Until my brother is found," he said, then turned his gaze to Charles. "And your daughter. Her safe return is my top priority."

Charles's only response was a slight incline of his head. Caesar was a terrible liar.

* * *

"Congratulations are in order, Alpha DuBois." The man strode forward, arms outstretched in greeting as he approached Caesar.

Caesar closed the distance and embraced him.

"Thank you." As they parted, their hands remained clasped on each other's forearms. "Caesar, please. Alpha DuBois was my late father."

"Well," the man said with a knowing smirk, "with his unfortunate demise and your brother's transgressions, the title is yours. Has the ceremony been performed?"

Caesar stiffened, his body reacting before his words. It had been a little over a month—too soon for the Rite of Selene. He would have to wait for the next full moon before the official crowning. The delay weakened his position. Without the ceremony, he was little more than a placeholder, his authority easily questioned.

Damien chuckled. "I'll take that as a 'no.' You are aware that without official recognition by your pack, we can't move forward with any present or past agreements."

"I'm aware," Caesar replied, irritation creeping into his tone.

"But that doesn't mean you and I can't talk business." Damien's gaze flicked toward Hera, lifting his champagne flute in her direction. "Your sister—Hera." He smiled. "Your father and I were discussing an arrangement between her and my cousin, Alexander. I assume those talks will continue once you're crowned?" He took a slow sip of his drink, eyes glinting with mischief.

Caesar's expression darkened. "No." His voice was firm, final. "Assume nothing, brother."

Damien chuckled, unfazed by Caesar's shift in demeanor.

"It's tradition for the next alpha to finish the dealings of the previous one."

Caesar arched an eyebrow.

"As you've so graciously pointed out, I haven't been officially recognized. That means I can't move forward with—how did you put it?—'present nor past agreements.'"

The tall Russian smirked.

"I'm willing to overlook certain… difficulties. Depending on what you have to offer."

Caesar exhaled sharply, feigning amusement.

"You want to discuss arrangements, now? At my wedding reception?" He clicked his tongue. "Shame on you for being so… rude."

The dark-haired Russian laughed, unbothered.

"Weddings are nothing more than a front for business. Since stepping through the door, I've overheard at least five different deals being made. So, let's get to it, shall we?" He lifted his glass to his lips, taking a slow sip.

Caesar studied him for a moment. Damien was brash, young. He had ascended to the rank of alpha at twenty-one, and though he had only held his position for two years, he was already someone to be respected. Feared. He was someone Caesar could do business with.

"Fine. I'll go first." Caesar leaned in slightly. "I'm sure you already know what I want. The deal we previously discussed—move forward with rounding up the necessary players for the Federation, and you can tell your cousin she's as good as his bride."

"I figured as much. But since we're starting fresh, I'd like to make an amendment to the previous deal regarding your sister."

Caesar quirked an eyebrow, intrigued by this unexpected turn—and how he might twist it to his advantage.

"Go on."

Damien met his gaze evenly.

"I want to restructure the arrangement. Instead of my cousin, I propose a marriage between myself and your sister."

Caesar's expression didn't waver, but his mind worked quickly.

"That would mean, once I'm officially recognized as alpha, I'd have to break with tradition—to overturn my late father's decision." He leaned back slightly. "Now, tell me, how do you think I'd be viewed if I went back on a blood-sealed agreement?"

Damien shrugged, entirely unbothered.

"How you look is of no concern to me. If you want my cooperation, that's my price."

Caesar exhaled through his nose, shaking his head.

"Then I'll require more." His voice was firm. "This wasn't just a conversation between men—papers were signed, binding papers, sealed in blood. If you want me to tear that apart, I'll need more than just your word that you'll do your part."

Damien flicked an invisible speck of lint from his sleeve, looking wholly uninterested. "Such as?"

"I need trackers. Not the ones your coven employs—your personal trackers." Caesar's voice dropped slightly. "And a mercenary. Not just that—I need you to handle the Egyptians."

At that, Damien's gaze sharpened.

"Ahmad has gone back on his deal," Caesar continued. "He's stirring up trouble in North Africa. And he's never been the type to keep his word."

Damien chuckled. "You ask a lot for a third born."

Caesar stepped closer, his eyes narrowing.

"You forget, Hera is the only female DuBois born to an alpha. Yesterday's price is not today's price, brother."

Damien clicked his glass against Caesar's, the sound sharp.

"Expect my trackers here by the end of the week. As for the Egyptians, consider it handled."

Caesar didn't hesitate.

"The mercenary?"

"All of my trackers are mercenaries, brother." Damien's smirk was knowing. "So, once the traitors, as you call them, are found, what would you like to have done with them?"

Caesar nodded, his smile widening. He quickly through a glance over Damien's shoulder to his new wife Evelyn hoping he could garner her attention. But she was shrouded the young ambitious women clawing for favor. He focused on the man in front of him.

"Let them do what mercenaries do." He extended his hand. "Hera is as good as your bride." He clasped Damien's hand firmly. "Welcome to the family."

The two men parted once the discussion was finished. Neither of them were big on small talk.

Hera approached, waiting until Damien was out of earshot. The alpha of the Russian coven had already started entertaining a small group of women who had gathered around the exotic foreigner. Hera hooked her arm through her brother's.

"What was that about?" she asked, her gaze drifting to Damien.

As if sensing her attention, Damien locked eyes with her and raised his glass in silent acknowledgment. Hera hissed under her breath. The reaction was almost instinctive.

Caesar caught the exchange and couldn't help but laugh. His baby sister's reaction was as adorable as it was telling. He was certain the two would clash—he was willing to bet money on it.

"He's an asshole." Hera muttered under her breath; her voice low but pointed.

"Well, that asshole is going to help us find our brother."

Hera looked up at him, her voice tinged with doubt. "And he will bring him home? To us?"

Caesar took a long sip from his glass.

"Something like that," he muttered, a dark chuckle escaping as he lowered his glass. "Although I can't promise he'll be in one piece."

Hera's brow furrowed, her gaze shifting uneasily.

"What does that mean?"

Caesar's expression hardened, the tone of his voice growing more serious.

"Once Armand is found, they'll kill him. I've given the order."

Hera's eyes widened in horror.

"The council agreed to this? What about the High Table? He has to stand trial."

He turned fully to face her, his body looming over hers.

"He killed our parents. He's the reason for all of this upheaval."

Hera's voice trembled out of anger as she asked, "Why didn't you ask me first?"

Caesar's eyes flashed with coldness.

"Because I don't have to, Hera. You're a third born, and a female. Don't forget your place."

She sighed, sadness settling over her like a heavy cloak. His words stung more than she cared to admit. She wanted to shift the topic, but the weight of the conversation pressed on.

Initially, Hera had only come to wish him and Evelyn well. She had intended to let her brother know she would be leaving in the morning to return to California. She had stayed long enough to grieve. But now, the walls seemed to be closing in, and old temptations—ones she thought she had left behind—were creeping back in beckoning her to partake.

"Congratulations," Hera offered, a weak smile tugging at her lips. The knowledge that Caesar wanted to kill their older brother deflated her, but it also sparked a simmering rage within.

"Well, I suspect in a month or so, I'll be extending those sentiments to you as well."

Hera's brows furrowed deeply, meeting in the middle.

Caesar noticed her confusion and smirked. He lifted his glass and gestured toward Damien.

"Damien has asked for your hand in marriage. I've consented."

Hera's eyes widened, her mouth twisting into a snarl.

"No," she hissed, her voice low and fierce.

Caesar rolled his eyes, his patience wearing thin. A few weeks in, and he felt no one respected his authority. He knew he'd have to make a change, but now wasn't the time.

"It's done, sister. You might as well start searching for dresses and rounding up your sorority sisters."

"No." Hera shook her head vehemently. "Father was talking with Alexander, his cousin. That was the agreement. I will not marry him."

"Father isn't here." Caesar's tone sharpened. "Besides, the deal with Alexander—a fifth born with no power—is off."

"What about the beta of the Westland Coven, Boris?"

"That's over, as well." Caesar's voice was firm and unyielding. "Sister, I'm not going to explain myself to you. Damien is a fine man, a respected and powerful alpha. He has influence. A strong bloodline. You should be grateful. I'm looking out for you, not giving you away to a barely known beta or someone of lower rank. Your name alone is worth more than that. We can do better, and I did."

He raised the glass, preparing to take another sip, when Hera slapped it from his hand. The sharp sound of glass hitting the floor echoed in the room. Several guests gasped. The older ones looked on in horror, while the younger crowd giggled, the bolder ones pulling out their phones to snap photos, raising them high in the air.

All eyes were on them, including Damien's. The young alpha watched with a smirk; his interest piqued. If it weren't for propriety, he would've thrown her on one of the tables and ravished her.

Caesar stepped closer, his presence dominating hers. He leaned in, his voice a low whisper in her ear. The tone was deadly.

"I'll take your tantrum as a result of grief and let this offense slide.

But be careful and be thankful I didn't rip your throat out."

Hera straightened, meeting his gaze. His eye had darkened, its depth swirling with danger. She had never seen him like this before—ferocious, almost unrecognizable. She realized now wasn't the time to push the issue. The proper moment would present itself, and she would be ready.

Without another word, Hera turned on her heel, ignoring the whispers that followed, and hurried toward the exit.

Evelyn stood across the room, her gaze shifting from her husband to her retreating sister-in-law. The unease in her chest grew. If Caesar couldn't hold it together, then she would need to make sure she had options—options that would keep not only her safe but her children as well.

Caesar straightened, his gaze sweeping across the room. A slow smile spread across his face, his canines barely visible beneath his top lip. The partygoers quickly took their cue, returning to their drinks. Their conversations dropped to hushed whispers. The mood shifted from festive to heavy as they kept glancing over their shoulders at him. The tension hung heavier than the Alabama humidity forming a curtain around them.

The Russian had watched the scene play out. Hera's little tantrum arousing him. Damien would find his fiancé's whereabouts and pay the young woman a visit.

2

Healing

"Girl," Leslie stumbled into the room, juggling several bags of ammonia. "The people gave me looks at self-checkout. They think I'm trying to hide a body."

Amelia rushed forward, relieving her of some of the bags.

"Well, technically, bodies."

Leslie narrowed her eyes.

"Cute. So why do you need all this again?"

"It's to mask our scent." Amelia through over her shoulder as she headed to the small kitchen area.

Leslie planted a hand on her hip.

"Okay, okay, you really need to explain this to me again." She flicked a long braid over her shoulder and followed after Amelia.

"I will. But first, I need to check on Armand."

Over the past few weeks, Armand had improved, but not enough. If the scouts found him, he wouldn't be able to defend himself. And if they found her? They wouldn't let her walk away. She'd seen too much. Heard too much.

And his brother—he wouldn't stop until the job was finished. Until they were both dead.

She found Armand by the window, his gaze locked on the darkened sky. He didn't turn when she entered, but she caught the glint of unshed tears in his eyes. She wouldn't mention them.

"Are you okay?" she asked, stepping closer.

He turned suddenly, wrapping her in his arms. She could feel the tension in him, the silent need to grasp something real.

"You know we can't stay here forever," he murmured against her hair. "It's too dangerous for your friend."

Amelia nodded. "I know. But I still think you're too weak—"

He pulled away, jaw tightening. She wasn't wrong. He wouldn't be fully healed until the next full moon—nearly a month away. Until then, they'd have to keep hiding, slipping through the shadows, moving only during the day.

"What's next?" she asked, standing by the bed, watching him.

"We need to know what my brother is planning." He hesitated, then exhaled sharply. "Do you know any seers?"

The question surprised her. Armand had never put much faith in the magic of the Night Wolves. But desperation had a way of making believers out of skeptics.

Amelia sighed. She wasn't sure how to tell him, but she knew someone, or rather a few techniques, that would help.

"Yes, I can do it. I think I can, at least."

She ran her hand through her hair out of nervousness. Her gift was still something she struggled to accept, something she hadn't yet learned to control.

"I have the ability. My aunt tried to help me nurture it over the years. She taught me spells, showed me how to reach across the veil. We were making a breakthrough before my mother kicked her out." Amelia hesitated. "I can try to go deeper, to see what we need to do."

She watched Armand, waiting for a reaction.

"Why didn't you tell me?"

13

His voice was softer than she expected. He wasn't angry—just hurt. He had shared everything with her. His assumption there were no more secrets left between them was wrong. With his brother's betrayal and everything he'd learned about his father, he couldn't help but wonder what else she was keeping from him. Was everyone like this? Did everyone keep secrets?

"Well, we haven't exactly had time to sit down and chat about magic. Or anything else, really."

She wiggled her eyebrows, and the tension in the room cracked. Armand exhaled a short laugh. It was nice feeling something other than rage.

"Okay," he said. "Is there a certain time you can, you know..." He waved a hand vaguely at the room, glancing at the ceiling. "See?" His lips quirked. "Forgive me, Amelia, but I've never believed in this stuff. I don't know what to do or say."

"No, I don't think so. When Aunt Nancy and I did readings, it worked at any time of day." She bit her bottom lip, letting it plop back out. "But... I am more sensitive during the day."

Armand only nodded. He wasn't sure about any of this. But if she believed, then he was willing to try.

"I don't need much. The setup is simple," she said. "Let me get Leslie. Give us about ten minutes, then come to the kitchen, okay?"

"Sure."

He watched Amelia leave before turning back to the window. A deep exhaustion settled into his bones, heavier than before. Since regaining enough strength to keep his eyes open on his own, he hadn't slept.

Waiting, he absently traced the scar across his chest with his middle finger. The memory of the wound lingered it was the closest he had ever come to death, and he was still feeling the weight of it, not just in his body, but in his mind as well.

A presence at the door pulled him from his thoughts. He turned, locking eyes with large, dark brown ones.

Leslie had tried to move quietly, as if staying silent could make all of this less real. Maybe if she didn't make a sound, she could convince herself it was all just a bad, strange dream.

But when his gaze landed on her, she flinched.

She quickly remembered why she was there and gestured for him to follow with a small flick of her hand. As he approached, she stepped back. Fear still clung to her, though its grip had loosened over the past week.

The small kitchen and living room were dim, lit only by two white candles burning in the center of a glass table. Shadows flickered against the walls. Armand's eyes swept the space before he took a seat across from Amelia.

Leslie sank onto a beanbag, cradling a glass of wine. Given the situation, Armand figured they'd all need something stronger.

Amelia slid her hands onto the table, palms up, her expression expectant. He hesitated, then lowered his hands into hers. The moment their skin touched; her lashes fluttered shut as if weighed down.

She exhaled slowly, focusing, reaching. Her voice dropped to a low murmur as she began the chant—the one used to call on the ancestors. She nudged at his aura, feeling for something beyond the veil. A tingle crawled up her spine. The spirit that stirred wasn't the usual one she connected with. But, it felt known.

Then—

"Son."

The voice was different. It was heavier tinged with an accent he associated with comfort. Her words soothing the little cuts his father's often left behind.

"My little Armie."

A sharp sting burned behind his eyes. He knew that voice. Knew that name.

"Mom?"

"Yes, my son. I am so sorry. Forgive me."

Armand's breath hitched. His mother. The warmth of her voice sent a painful ache through his chest, but it was tainted with sorrow.

"You did nothing wrong," he choked out. "All of it was Father. This is his fault. Caesar—" His voice broke as hot tears trailed down chiseled cheeks.

Across from him, Amelia—animated by the spirit—lowered her gaze, defeat flickering in her features before she met his eyes again.

"But I have, son. I have. Your father isn't the only one to blame."

"But—" Armand began, but a sharp hiss silenced him.

Glass shattered.

Leslie had moved. The wine glass lay in pieces at the base of the beanbag, crimson liquid spreading across the floor like blood. The shift in energy—the voice that wasn't Amelia's—was enough to send her scrambling behind the couch. She peeked over its edge, then stole a glance at the ceiling, as if expecting something unnatural to descend. Her wide eyes darted back to the couple at the table.

"Not all of this is about Samuel. Or the Coven," his mother's voice continued, solemn. "Your father killed Samuel. That much is true. But I murdered my sister—for the same reason Caesar wants to kill you."

Armand tensed, instinct driving him to pull away, but Amelia's grip tightened around his hands.

"No!" the inhabited body before him warned, nails digging into his skin. "Contact cannot be broken, or the connection will be lost."

Armand swallowed hard.

"Listen to me. You have to move fast. Your brother is advancing his plans. He wants you dead. Amelia as well. And I fear for your sister—if she continues to support your safe return, if she defies him, Hera will suffer his wrath."

His mother's voice wavered, but the urgency only sharpened.

16

"Caesar will not stop, Armand. He has to be stopped. You know what must be done."

A slow, resigned nod. His gaze fell to the table, then lifted to Amelia—no, to the ghost wearing her face.

"The twins," she pressed. "His ambition will not only destroy him, but them as well. If he continues on this path, he will burn everything to get what he wants. And he will have it—if you fail to stop him."

A muscle in Armand's jaw twitched.

"I will stop him, Mother."

Silence stretched between them. There was much left unsaid.

"You must kill him, Armand. There is no other way."

The candlelight flickered; shadows danced wildly across the walls as her final words settled into his bones.

"You must fight his darkness… with your own."

Armand hissed, leaning closer.

"I can't kill him. Despite everything he's done. He's my brother—he's sick. You and Dad should have helped him."

"We tried our best. Despite his illness it won't stop. He won't stop.

"He needs help, Mother. What you're asking me to do is impossible."

"Both of you cannot live, son. It has already been written. The Great Wolf's will shall be done."

A fresh crack split his heart. The weight of her words made his stomach churn. One of them had to die. The finality of it sickened him—but deep down, something darker stirred. *Vengeance.* It had become a hunger gnawing at his insides; a fire that burned through grief. Caesar had shattered their family's fragile peace. Nothing would ever be the same.

Aside from rage, there wasn't any other emotion left.

"He will seek out the Two Sisters. Witches. Skinwalkers that feed on children. Twins. He will go to them for power. But their magic is not gifted from above—it is taken from below. And they will demand something pure in return."

Armand stiffened. His hands curled into fists.

"Then how am I supposed to defeat him? I won't just roll over and let him destroy us. I won't let him harm Hera."

He inclined his head toward Amelia.

His mother's voice softened.

"Of course not, son. I would never expect you to. But you must perform the Blood Oath. The Mother of the Waters will give you the strength you need."

"Where do I find her?"

"She knows the way."

Silence thickened the air between them. Amelia's lids grew heavy, her vision unfocused. The hazy film clouding her eyes lifted, fading to their natural hue.

She blinked, disoriented.

"Did anything happen?"

Amelia released Armand's hands, glancing between him and Leslie.

From behind the couch, Leslie slowly emerged. She hesitated approaching and stopping just shy of the table, eyes wide, mouth parted in stunned disbelief.

"Yeah, IT happened. Whatever that was—it was fucking amazing!" A slow grin spread across her lips as she nodded, braids bouncing around her face.

Amelia frowned.

"She said—" she trailed off hoping one of them would take over. She remembered Armand's mother and the words that she'd used her tongue to speak. As well as the words that Hemesh told Amelia not to reveal.

Not yet.

Armand took the pregnant pause as his cue to take over.

"My mother mentioned something about the Two Sisters and then a

Blood Oath and the Mother of the Waters. She said you would know the way."

Amelia shifted uncomfortably. She'd heard about the witches. You didn't mess with them. Unless you were willing to offer a blood sacrifice, you stayed away.

As for the Mother of the Waters, she knew the way, at least in theory. She had read about the ritual and even practiced a mock layout using popsicle sticks. But she wasn't sure if this was something she was ready for.

3

New Information

C harles had uncovered new revelations about his friend—and about Hemesh. This wasn't as simple as it seemed. Armand hadn't killed anyone. Aside from himself, the Council, and a handful of others at the High Table, most remained convinced Armand was the culprit.

The car hugged a sharp curve. His grip on the steering wheel slipped. *Was he next?* He had to be. The way Caesar's goons lingered near him at meetings and casual gatherings—it was only a matter of time. Like Spencer, he too would disappear. His only fear was for Amelia, wife, and two sons. They would be caught in the crossfire. Collateral damage.

His aunt had always been difficult to find. She believed in the old ways of the wolf and never put down roots since she left home at sixteen. At four foot eleven, Maxine was a force of unnatural power even taking down a bear alone. But she was constantly on the move, slipping through life like smoke. But after speaking with his cousin, who led him to a stepbrother, then to a son of Maxine's deceased brother, then to her eldest daughter—finally, he had a lead.

The daughter wasn't exactly sure where her mother was these days.

Maxine sent letters from previous places she stayed, never lingering in one spot for too long. But someone knew. Someone who stayed close. Someone she had mentored in the ways of black magic. Elnora had given him another lead—a protégé. That lead turned into a direct number to Maxine. And now, he was in front of a small, decrepit store. He stepped out of the car, taking in his surroundings. His attention lingered on the small crowd.

A group of thugs loitered nearby, their postures straightening the moment they spotted him. Hands rested on the waistbands of sagging jeans. The tallest one held up a hand in warning, eyeing him with suspicion. Charles met his gaze, then gave a subtle nod. A beat passed before the tension eased. The man stepped back, and the group returned to their dice game, their sodas rattling on a battered, makeshift table.

"Madame Maxine's inside." The man jerked his chin toward the weather-beaten door.

Charles hesitated. His grip on his keys tightened.

"She good, don't worry." The man's eyes flicked to the sleek Aston Martin, easily reading Charles' unease.

Charles exhaled.

"Thanks, man."

He headed inside. The scent of fresh blood hit him first—raw, metallic, overwhelming. His stomach clenched and he let out a low growl. He hadn't eaten since the night before. His mind had been too occupied with death—his friend's mangled body, the man's wife's lifeless form. But it was the children that haunted him. Spencer's grandchildren, their limbs scattered like discarded dolls.

"Charlie?" A voice called from the back room.

He stepped forward, crossing the threshold into thick, suffocating darkness. He stilled, letting his eyes adjust.

Candles flared to life, their flames licking at the shadows. At the far end of the room, a woman sat the deep violet silk of the table cloth complimenting dark brown skin.

"Aunt Maxine?"

"Little Charlie!" She grinned, revealing a gap where a tooth used to be.

"I haven't been called that in years."

"You'll always be Little Charlie to me." Her gaze swept over him, her expression darkening. "Your spirit is heavy."

Her head moved from side to side searching for the voices.

"The spirits have already spoken. You want answers—about Maximillian, Hemesh. I warned you about them decades ago."

She beckoned him closer. He didn't argue, stepping toward the small table.

Maxine stretched out her hands, palms up.

"Did you bring anything of theirs?" Her fingers twitched impatiently.

Without a word, he placed a sapphire hairpin in her right hand, a blood-soaked scrap of Maximillian's shirt in her left. Maxine inhaled deeply, then released a slow, measured breath. Her fingers tightened around the items.

She moaned as the first drop of blood fell to the floor. The sapphire hairpin plunged into the side of Maximillian's neck made her hiss. There was more blood followed by a fight between two brothers then a gunshot. But wait…her great niece saved the dying Armand taking him away to safety.

Her eyes snapped open.

"Give me your hands."

Charles obeyed, placing his hands over hers.

The moment his fingers made contact, the visions seized him, dragging him under.

A rush of chaos. A blur of movement. A room thick with screams. Armand. Caesar. Hemesh. Maximillian. Evelyn. His daughter. Charles stood frozen in the corner, powerless to stop what was coming.

His eyes snapped open as he yanked his hands away from his aunt's clammy grasp. Slowly, he met her gaze—dark, cloudy brown eyes locked onto his.

"Seen enough?" Maxine's grin was sharp, challenging. "There's more. A lot more."

Charles exhaled shakily and shook his head. He'd seen more than enough. His daughter was alive. So was Armand. That was a start. Caesar was behind everything—the packages, the threats—but without proof, the council wouldn't listen. Without their support, there was no stopping Caesar from taking control. He pushed to his feet and dropped a wad of cash onto the table.

"Thanks, Aunt Maxie," he said. His shirt clung uncomfortably to his back, sweat cooling against his skin. His skull throbbed where she had forced the images into his mind.

Maxine handed the items back to him, her expression softer now. The clouded haze in her eyes had cleared.

"Aunt Maxie?" she mused, tucking the money away. "Haven't been called that in over forty years." Her gaze sharpened. "This has shaken you."

Charles swallowed hard. It had. He never got over what had been done to Samuel. The man's ghost still haunted him. He didn't need any more unwanted visitors in his dreams.

"Yes," he admitted.

"Karma keeps score, Charles."

"I know," he murmured. He turned and stepped through the beaded curtain, disappearing into the night.

"You'll be in touch," she called after him.

He heard her. But didn't answer.

Outside, he nodded once to the tall man at the old pump, then slid into his car. Gravel crunched beneath the tires as he pulled onto the road. He knew the truth now. The real problem was getting the council to believe it—and stopping Caesar before it was too late.

* * *

A soft knock at her bedroom door drew her attention. Hera hesitated, slipping off her headphones. *Had she imagined it?* Another. The door was barely cracked open. She swung her legs off the bed and padded over, pulling it wider. Lupa stood there, head bowed in quiet deference.

"Yes, Lupa?"

"The Alpha is here to see you," she said.

Hera rolled her eyes returning to the bed and settled onto her knees.

"My brother is technically not the Alpha," she muttered. "You don't have to call him that."

Her words hung in the air. Lupa had already left to fetch the unwanted visitor. She took a deep breath, closing her eyes as heavy footsteps echoed down the hall. A slow, mocking voice followed.

"Ah, isn't that a beautiful sight to behold? Though, when my women kneel, they're usually on the floor."

Hera's eyes snapped open.

"Fuck! What do you want?" she snapped, shifting into a cross-legged position. "If I'd known it was you, I would've told security to throw you out. Why are you even here?"

Damien smirked.

"I've come to see my fiancée." His tone was smooth, casual—too casual. "I heard you were denied travel and hadn't left your room in the past few days. Thought you might've taken ill. I came to see if I could be of any comfort."

Hera snorted. "Even if I were on my deathbed, I wouldn't send for you."

Damien placed both hands over his heart in mock offense. "That hurts."

"Yeah, right."

Silence stretched between them, tense and unspoken. Hera was the first to break it.

"Seriously, Damien. Why are you here?"

"To talk." He adjusted the cuffs of his sleeves, unbothered. "With everything going on, and my business here wrapping up, it's time. You and I should be married—let's say in a week or two. We'll have another ceremony once we're settled in Russia."

She stiffened.

"I'm not marrying you."

"I wasn't asking." His smirk deepened, grating on her nerves. "I'm telling you. I simply came to extend the courtesy of letting you pick the date and time." He shrugged. "Night, day, weekend—I'm not particular."

Hera's clenched her jaw.

"I'm not marrying you. When they discussed an alliance, it was supposed to be with Alexander. Not you." Her glare darkened. "I would never dream of marrying an Alpha. Let alone you."

Damien chuckled, tilting his head.

"Oh, don't be so modest. My cousin is my Beta, after all. And let's be honest—someone like you would die of boredom with Alex within two years."

"Unlike my brother, I don't care about that. I want a simple life—away from the politics of the coven."

Damien laughed, a deep, rumbling sound as he clutched his stomach through his dark blue silk shirt. Hera's gaze flicked, unbidden, to the way the fabric stretched over his taut frame.

"Keep telling yourself that lie long enough, and you just might believe it." He strolled through her room, fingers grazing the dolls lined up along the walls. He tapped one, making its head wobble.

"Creepy." He smirked. "When you move to Russia, you're ditching this doll shit. That's one of my boundaries—no dolls."

Hera crossed her arms. "Tell yourself whatever you like. And who says I'm moving to Russia?"

"I do." He glanced at her, amusement flickering in his dark eyes. "Once we're married, surely you don't think you'll stay here with your brother while madness slowly claims him."

"I'm not staying with anyone," she shot back. "I'm going back to California."

Damien scoffed. "Ah, I see. So you're just going to hole up in your dead parents' penthouse?" He threw up his hands. "Yeah, because nothing screams 'well-adjusted' like isolating yourself in a ghost town of memories."

Hera's patience snapped. She tossed her headphones onto the bed and stalked toward him, stopping just inches away.

"Let's get a few things straight," she said, voice cold. "One—don't touch my dolls. They're collector's items."

Damien smirked. He wouldn't say it aloud, but her fire was beginning to turn him on.

"Okay," he murmured.

"Two—the wedding, proposal, or whatever little shady side deal you and my brother cooked up, is off. And three—I want the original deal with Alexander. Got it? I like Alexander. He'll make a good mate."

She planted her hands on her hips, chin lifted defiantly.

Damien almost laughed. Her attempt to lay down the law was admirable—cute, even. But at some point, she'd have to be brought to heel. The real challenge was how to do it without breaking her spirit.

He yanked her closer, pulling her flush against him. Hera squirmed, her breath hitching as she felt the unmistakable hardness between them. Heat coiled in her core, her body betraying her even as her mind rebelled.

"I could take you right now," Damien murmured, his voice dropping to a low, ragged whisper. "Hard. Bite you. Mark you. That's exactly what I'm going to do—mark you, make sure everyone knows you're mine."

His free hand slipped beneath the hem of her shorts, stopping just shy of where she ached the most. Her breathing deepened. She tensed—not from fear, but from arousal. A familiar disgust slithered through her. It always happened. And it always left her frustrated. Enraged.

Damien pressed his nose to her forehead, inhaling deeply, his low hum vibrating through his chest. He wanted her—badly. But he would wait. Restraint wasn't his strong suit, but the anticipation would make it all the sweeter when she finally gave in.

Because she would.

His conviction wasn't just arrogance—it was an assessment. A selfish one, sure, but honest. She'd tire of his cousin. Of the dull, predictable life Alexander had carved out for himself.

"It's okay." His lips barely ghosted against her skin. "You don't have to pretend you don't like this. I know you do." A smirk tugged at his mouth. "I've heard all the rumors, Hera. The women. The ropes. The pain." He tilted his head, watching her reaction. "You're like me. You just won't admit it."

Hera shook.

"I don't know what you've heard, but I am nothing like you."

Damien chuckled, dark and knowing.

"For once, you're right. We are different." He let his fingers drag along her thigh before pulling away. "I embrace who I am—the pain I enjoy inflicting. You?" He tsked. "You sit in your room, locked away, repressed. It's a long way from putting sorority girls in comas."

Her expression hardened. That part of her—the one she wanted erased—had no place in this conversation.

"You don't have to talk about it," he said, amusement curling at the edges of his words. "News travels fast, especially when a wolf is being considered to join my pack." His gaze gleamed with intrigue. "I know more about you than you think. Which is why I'm so... fascinated."

Hera clenched her fists, the urge to strike him warring with the knowledge that any reaction might only fuel his arousal—and hers. If he pushed further, she wasn't sure she could resist. Her curiosity of him simmered beneath her irritation. His arrogance and womanizing grated on her, but still, something about him kept her rooted in place. She refused to let him win.

"You should leave." Her voice was taut, laced with the same tension tightening his jaw. Damien smirked to himself. Stubborn. But she was interested. That was a start. For him, it was enough.

His grip loosened as his fingers trailed down her thigh. She jerked back, arms folding across her chest like a shield.

"Yes, I should." He slid his hands into his pockets, watching as she sank onto the bed. "But I'll be back. Dinner."

"No."

"I wasn't asking." His hand found the doorknob. "Tomorrow. Seven-thirty. I'll be here around seven." He waggled his eyebrows and winked before slipping through the cracked door.

She groaned, collapsing backward into her pillows. He was an arrogant ass—but damn if that wasn't sexy as hell.

It was nearing nine when Lupa returned, announcing yet another visitor.

Hera grabbed her robe, draping it over the thin silk lounge set. Half annoyed, half intrigued, she expected Damien. Anticipation curled in her stomach as she followed Lupa. Better to meet him somewhere other than her bedroom—especially with the way he pushed boundaries. If he did it again, she wasn't sure she'd resist.

Stepping into the room, her breath hitched—not Damien.

Charles Anaheim, her father's closest friend, stood at the center, his expression pinched with worry.

"Mr. Anaheim?" Her brow furrowed. "What do I owe the pleasure?"
Shouldn't he be helping search for her brother and his daughter?
His gaze flicked toward the three young men lingering in the corners.
"Is there somewhere we can talk? Privately?"

"We can talk here. I mean, it's just me and the staff." She glanced around. The coven workers were a constant presence—so much so that she had learned to ignore them over the years.

Charles shook his head.

"It's important. I'd prefer to discuss this in private."

She hesitated, then nodded, taking his elbow and leading him down the hall to her father's private study. The room had long been used for sensitive discussions with high-ranking coven members—conversations she had no business overhearing as a child. It was also where she once walked in on her parents arguing, their voices sharp enough to cut through the heavy wooden door.

Closing it behind them, she turned to face him. "What's this about?"

Annoyance prickled at the edges of her voice. She had hoped it was Damien. She knew little about Charles beyond the fact that he was a founding member and her father's most trusted advisor.

"Hera, please sit." He gestured toward a chair.

She remained standing, arms crossed.

Charles exhaled, his expression unreadable. He might as well get it out.

"What do you know about the manner of your parents' deaths? Or how it came to such a tragic end?"

Her fingers twitched as she dropped her arms to her sides.

"Nothing much. Just what my brother told me." Her voice hardened. "You do realize Caesar lost his eye that night?"

She squared her shoulders. "Excuse my tone, but can you just tell me why you're here? The suspense is—honestly—irritating."

Charles sighed, dropping his hand to his side. No sense in dragging it out.

"Your mother killed your father. Then herself."

The words struck like a physical blow. A punch to the ribs. A sudden, violent shattering of the world she thought she knew. Her body locked; her mind blank. The story had always been simple: Armand was responsible. That was what she had been told. That was what she believed. She couldn't breathe. Her diaphragm seized, refusing to function and her legs felt heavy.

Charles reached for her, his grip firm around her forearms.

"Sit. There's more."

This time, she didn't resist.

"Go on."

She remembered how to speak, but the words felt hollow, devoid of meaning. *Go on.* She had spoken to them so casually, like an irritated parent urging a child to hurry up and finish. But now, their weight pressed against her chest and it was suffocating.

Charles did as requested, unbuttoning his blazer with stiff fingers. It felt like a straitjacket. Damp fabric clung to him, and a sheen of sweat glistened beneath the overhead lights. And so, he went on.

He unraveled the truth—or what he claimed was the truth—contradicting everything her brother had sworn to her. His words chipped away at the foundation she had built her beliefs on, each revelation pulling her further onto unfamiliar, unstable ground.

When he finally fell silent, Hera stood. Her expression gave away nothing. Cold. Neutral.

"Leave." Her voice was even, but the threat beneath it was unmistakable. "And don't speak a word of this to anyone."

She threatened to go to her brother, to expose Charles as a traitor, a liar, a man spewing slanderous accusations against Caesar. She hadn't believed him. Couldn't. But doubt slithered into her mind, it was unwelcome and relentless.

Caesar warned her of this. Of councilmen who denied him his birthright. Of men like Anaheim, hungry for power, waiting for their moment to claim the throne. And with their father gone, nothing stood in their way.

It only took twenty minutes. Now, she was back in her room, the conversation looping in her mind like a cursed incantation.

Charles had laid out his so-called facts—his theory. He wouldn't reveal how he had come by this knowledge, but his claims fit too neatly with her brother's movements. The sudden push for her to marry Damien. Her hand in marriage nothing more than payment for services rendered.

Did Caesar need the Alpha for something? Or worse... did he have something on him? Hera shook her head, dismissing the thought.

The Russian wasn't sloppy. Even his mistakes were deliberate. If people knew things about Damien, it was because he wanted them to. Carefully curated. Controlled. The night stretched endlessly as she sat on her balcony, watching the streets stir at the earliest hint of dawn. She had to do something.

She just didn't know what.

4

Contingency Plan

E velyn awoke to an empty bed. It wasn't unusual—Caesar always had responsibilities that pulled him away—but she had once been a light sleeper, waking at his slightest movements. Since the pregnancy, though, everything was different. She had changed. He had changed.

Her husband had never been the doting type, not that she minded, but he had never been this cold. Not to her.

In the past weeks, their relationship became buried beneath layers of bitter frost. Evelyn felt her hope withering with each glacial breath between them. She couldn't endure this winter. Not this time.

She exhaled, pushing herself upright, one hand reaching for her phone while the other instinctively cradled her stomach. It wouldn't be long. She was nearing the end of her fifty-two-day gestation—another plight of wolf women. Not enough time to adjust, to prepare.

But she would make the call anyway.

The line barely rang before it connected.

"Ev, how's it going?" Her brother's voice carried its usual playful undertone.

Relief loosened the tightness in her chest. *Good. He's in a decent mood.*

"Can you talk?" she asked, rubbing slow circles over her belly.

"If I couldn't, I wouldn't have picked up."

There was a brief pause before he spoke again, "Go on, little sis, tell your big brother what's on your mind."

She was about to begin but was stopped by her brother.

"Ah, before we discuss any unpleasantness I must say congratulations. Suri and I apologize for missing the wedding—very unfortunate, truly. Trouble in the lower villages is keeping me occupied. But Mother and Father couldn't stop talking about how beautiful you were," he sighed.

She heard the familiar creak of his chair as he no doubt leaned back.

Evelyn decided to get straight to the point before her brother ventured off topic again.

"I need protection." Silence on the other end. She thought he had hung up.

Then, a quiet chuckle. "Sister, you know the rules. You belong to his pack now. Officially. I can't just swoop in. My interference alone would be grounds for war between the covens."

A pause.

"But," he continued voice laced with amusement, "as you well know, dear sister, I have never been one for rules."

He laughed, loud and uninhibited. Evelyn had to pull the phone away from her ear until the spell passed. Then, as quickly as it came, the laughter was gone, and when he spoke again, his voice was edged with something colder. Serious. His tone taking on a danger she had only heard once before.

"Why do you need protection, sister? Has Caesar done something? Is he beating you? I will come right away."

Tulsi's voice sharpened, edged with the kind of fury that could level cities. Evelyn knew if she didn't handle this carefully, her brother would drop everything and storm stateside, ready to rain down hellfire.

"No. He hasn't so much as raised his voice to me. No, it's just…"

she trailed off, throat tightening. She had never been good at this—at admitting fear.

A low chuckle rumbled through the receiver.

"You're worried about Armand's wrath. Given that you and Caesar orchestrated this mess, I'd say it's well-earned."

Her grip on the phone tightened. Her palms were damp. Wet. The device felt slippery in her grasp, and she feared she might drop it.

"Oh, sister," Tulsi continued, his laughter curling like smoke through the line. "News travels fast—even to us savages in the backcountry."

"This isn't funny." Her voice wavered, and to her horror, she realized she was on the verge of tears.

"You have every right to be afraid." His tone sobered just enough.

"Maximillian publicly named Armand his heir. With him still alive, and Caesar lacking the council's recognition, Armand still has a claim."

"But Armand killed his father and mother. Surely—"

His laughter cut her off. It was cold and carried with it a humiliating amusement.

"Sister, sister. This is why Father never wanted you reading those English novels. You think the Council actually cares about regicide?" Another pause followed by a dry chuckle.

"Ha. Darling, that is the way it's done. If Armand came back tomorrow, no one would oppose him. No, they'd welcome him with open arms—an image of a true alpha." He laughed again, and Evelyn shuddered. The sound was like glass scraping against a chalkboard.

She sucked in a breath, steadying herself.

"Yes, I know, but as you also know, brother, this situation puts me and my children at risk. I need to know that if shit goes left, I can count on you."

Silence. Then, a slow, measured sigh.

Tulsi wasn't sure if he could do anything. He wasn't sure if he wanted to. If Armand returned, demanding Caesar's blood—and the blood of his lineage—that would include Evelyn and their unborn children. Tulsi had no interest in making an enemy of the American coven. Not when his own country was already steeped in war. He was still locked in a power struggle with the neighboring villages.

He had his own battles to fight. His own scores to settle. Taking on a charity case was out of the question.

"If this doesn't end well, you and Caesar have no one to blame but yourselves." Tulsi's voice carried no malice, only certainty. He wouldn't offer false hope, nor would he make promises he had no intention of keeping.

Evelyn opened her mouth to argue, but stopped when Tulsi continued.

"The clauses Caesar is proposing are nearly identical to the nonsense you used to spout back home," he sighed heavily, shaking his head. "How did you get yourself into this, sister?" His voice held weight, but little sympathy.

"You talk as if I chose this," she whispered harshly, stepping closer to the window. "No one asked my opinion—not about coming here, not about marriage."

Tulsi chuckled, a sound laced with irony.

"Ah, but if you recall, Tessa had agreed to join the Americans and marry the younger brother. Then you stepped in and changed her mind."

"It was either be sent off to a foreign land or become wife number six to Don. The man's a tyrant. I wouldn't call that much of a choice."

"From your viewpoint, maybe not. But a choice was made." He paused briefly before he continued. "I understand why you picked Caesar. The American Coven has more money, more influence than Seychelles could ever dream of. But choices have consequences, sister. Now, you have to deal with the fallout."

She exhaled sharply. "So, I take this little talk of ours as your long-winded way of saying you won't help me?

"Now, now. Don't go putting words in my mouth." His tone was almost amused. "By the laws that govern us all, my hands are tied. But I will do what I can to keep you alive."

A beat of silence.

"I never did send a wedding present," he mused. "But I think I have the perfect gift. You can expect her to arrive by the end of the week."

"Her?" Evelyn frowned.

"Yes, her." His voice softened, but it carried an unspoken warning. "Now, don't question it—simply accept."

Before she could press further, Tulsi ended the call.

Evelyn exhaled, fogging up a small patch of the window as she slipped the phone into the pocket of her robe. She wasn't sure why, but she had faith in her brother. History hadn't given her much to go on, but he had always come through for their sister. She just hoped that same luck would extend to her.

* * *

Charles entered his home to darkness. His senses heightened. He wasn't alone an unsettling presence lurking nearby. The fine hairs on his arms stiffened like needles as he stepped further inside. The councilman anticipated an ambush. In the dim light of the dining room, he found his wife sitting at the table. Alone and alive.

Diane occupied the head seat, her only company a half-empty jug of moonshine. Sad mahogany eyes met his sable colored ones, rimmed with exhaustion and something else—something raw.

"Did you find… her? Amelia." Her words came out strained.

Her manicured hand trembled as she brought it to her face, lips

36

quivering. "My God," Diane wailed, squeezing her eyes shut. Charles shook his head, pulled out a chair, and sank into it.

"I didn't go to Maxine for that," he whispered, staring at his shaking hands. "Not specifically."

Diane's eyes snapped open, pupils blown wide. The whites had darkened, glossy like glass marred by storm clouds. The sharp crack of her palm against the wooden table made him jump.

"You drove out there to do what, exactly?" she demanded, voice edged with fire. She didn't wait for an answer, "surely, the man I married would be looking for our daughter! If it wasn't for Amelia, then why go out there? Why seek out the old woman?"

The glass in her hand was slammed down. The delicate stem snapped just below the bulb, sending a shard skittering across the table. Charles' eyes locked onto it before his gaze flicked up to her.

"I needed to know what happened to Max," he said, his voice rough. "I needed the whole story, Diane. There were too many missing pieces! The threats started months ago, then the packages came. This person—whoever they are—they knew things only Max and I should have known."

A sharp intake of breath. Diane turned toward him; her expression unreadable.

"Max? Everything is about Max! It has been for the past thirty years years of our marriage. I don't care about the past or what you two did! Lesser wolves have done worse for far weaker causes than flushing out a tyrant."

"He was my best friend, Diane. We grew up together. The past isn't just a memory—it's here, and it killed Max!"

"Yes, but Amelia is your daughter, Charles! Right now, she's lost! She's out there with Armand, and for all I know, she could be dead!" Diane's voice cracked as she hurled the bulb in her hand at him. It struck his chest with a dull thud before bouncing onto the table and shattering into jagged shards.

"Amelia is alive. I saw it all—Maxine showed me." His voice was steady, certain. "It's Caesar and Evelyn. They are behind all of this."

Diane let out a sharp breath, rubbing her hands over her face, smearing away the layer of oil that clung to her skin.

"I should have known that African bitch was involved. But thank God—our baby is still alive."

She pushed to her feet, moving to kneel beside him. "I'm sorry," she murmured, tracing her hands down his chest before sliding them up to cradle his face. Her lips brushed along his jaw, pressing soft, deliberate kisses up to his ear.

Charles caught her wrists, holding her still. His grip was firm but not cruel as he gently pushed her back.

"I will bring our daughter home," he vowed. "I will stop him and Evelyn. I will kill them if necessary."

His fingers tightened around her wrists, just for a moment.

"But you—get the boys. Pack your things. You all need to disappear. Tonight."

Diane's breath hitched. She stared at him, her eyes wide, searching his face.

"Where…" she trailed off, already knowing the usual places wouldn't be safe. Every property they owned was listed with the Coven. Finding them would be as simple as a record search.

Except for one. It was remote. Hidden.

"We could go—"

Charles lifted a hand, cutting her off.

"Don't tell me." His voice dropped, a quiet warning.

"I am a strong man, but torture… it's a powerful tool when wielded by the proper hands."

"Surely… they—surely, Caesar wouldn't stoop so low."

Charles exhaled, the weight of resignation settling in his voice.

"He already has. Frank was found—or, at least, what was left of him. Several pieces. His wife's body was mutilated. The grandkids too. And Pierce... he disappeared last night. Reynolds just sent word."

The room seemed to shrink around them. Whatever warmth remained in Diane's face drained away, her rich brown complexion dulling to an ashen hue.

Charles swallowed. The sound, barely audible but it still made her skin prickle. That feeling the panic curling in her gut caused her breath to hitch. She had felt this before over thirty years ago.

Charles inhaled deeply, his broad shoulders pulling back as if bracing for a storm. The shift in his posture, the quiet that settled over him. It was familiar. The solemn set of his jaw, the flicker of something raw in his eyes. Diane knew what was coming. She knew that look. A return to his old ways. His gaze was steady, dark with intent. The same look she hadn't seen since the bloody beginnings of the Coven. It was the look of a man who was about to get his paws dirty.

5

Ritual and Dissension Brewing

The bodies had been lying in the basement of Charles' practice since the engagement party, slowly surrendering to time. The stench of decay clung to the air, thick and inescapable.

Two of Caesar's henchmen stood off to the side. The taller one watched Charles through narrowed lids, his scrutiny sharp and unyielding. The older man, in contrast, stared straight ahead, feigning disinterest as Charles carried out the meager tasks permitted to him. But Charles knew better. The man's steely gray eyes—trained, calculating—never left him.

"I need to perform an autopsy," Charles muttered, reaching for a scalpel.

"No."

The word was curt, clipped. Rubber soles pressed against the cold floor as the taller guard stepped forward. Charles set the blade down slowly, deliberately, before raising his gaze to meet the man now standing inches from him.

"An autopsy is standard procedure when someone hasn't died of natural causes or fallen in a challenge," Charles said evenly. "Even we adhere to standard medical practice give or take a few *modifications.*

And this wound here—" he gestured toward Maximillian's partially covered body "this doesn't look natural."

The man stiffened; his irritation barely masked as he straightened his posture.

"I have my orders. The Alpha has decreed that no autopsy be performed. His father will not be further defiled—nor his memory."

Charles turned toward him fully, squaring his shoulders.

"Our Alpha is dead."

The young man stepped closer until their noses were nearly touching.

"The former Alpha is dead," he corrected, voice low. "Our Alpha—our rightful leader—stands alive and well."

Charles didn't think it was possible, but the man leaned in even closer. The scent of a fresh kill clung to his breath. It was pungent. Foul. Charles fought the urge to recoil as the stench settled thick, in his nostrils.

"Are you questioning the legitimacy of our Alpha?"

"No," Charles replied, his tone as steady as his pulse. "I'm simply stating the obvious. Maximillian is dead. Until the Rite of Selene is performed, we have no Alpha. The council holds all power, and as Second Chair, I have full authority to order an autopsy. That's Decree."

The young man said nothing, but his clenched jaw betrayed his anger. His nostrils flaring. The older guard remained still, standing at a calculated distance. His gaze never wavered, his face a mask of indifference. But Charles knew he was watching. Measuring. Waiting.

Charles made his decision. He would stand down...for now. Pressing further would get him nowhere.

The young man chuckled, the sound low and smug.

"Ah, it seems you've been out of the loop. Your absence hasn't gone unnoticed. The Council's power—along with the High Table's—has been suspended until further notice. That little detail is covered in the Decree. I'm sure you're well aware."

Charles masked his shock, rolling his shoulders back, lengthening his spine.

"So," the man continued, stepping away, "there will be no autopsy. Our Alpha—Caesar—has commanded it."

He gestured toward the bodies of Maximillian and Hemesh.

"Your time's up. Put them back in the fridge. The Crossing Over is scheduled for tomorrow evening. The maids will need time to prepare the bodies."

"If you say so." Charles smirked, though the expression didn't reach his eyes. He pulled the sheet over Maximillian and rolled him toward the freezer, repeating the process with Hemesh. Without another word, he turned and left.

He needed answers. How the hell had they let Caesar become a dictator?

* * *

"We're busting our asses for nothing," Winston muttered, shifting back into human form as he leaned against a towering poplar tree. His breath curled in the cold air.

"If those two had any brains, they'd be long gone. Hell, probably out of the country by now."

James shifted next, his sleek, dark brown fur rippling away to reveal tan skin. He rolled his shoulders, adjusting to the change.

"Our orders are clear. We find Armand."

"In the middle of the damn woods?" Winston scoffed, throwing up his hands. "That dick isn't even the real Alpha. So what if Armand killed his old man? I mean half the alphas got their start through regicide."

He dragged a finger across his throat for emphasis.

James exhaled hard, scuffing his bare foot against the damp earth. Pieces of bark scattered under his weight.

"Look, Win, I'm just saying—we have orders. We have a job. We're scouts. And our job is to…" He trailed off, hesitating, searching for something—anything—better than the obvious. But the truth hung between them, heavy and inescapable.

"Scout." Winston's voice dripped with sarcasm, cutting through the cool night air.

James ignored the jab. "You ever think about… more?"

Winston pushed off the tree with a sigh.

"More what, James?"

"Being more than a scout. More than this. All the power's concentrated at the top. Shouldn't we be more of a democracy than an oligarchy?"

Winston let out a low whistle.

"Ooh, big words. Big words. Now where'd you pick up all this political talk? Thought you were all about serving the coven. That's all you cared about when you joined four years ago. What changed?"

James rolled his eyes.

"That was before the veil was lifted. You know—after Canada." He stretched his arms over his head, staring up at the sky.

Winston scoffed.

"You picked all that up in what—eight weeks?"

"Yes, and then some." James' grin widened as they walked along the narrow, overgrown trail. "They even gave me some reading material."

"Right. You were sent there to train with Canadian scouts. And all outside reading has to be approved by the Coven Matriarch."

"Hey, what Hemesh didn't know at the time didn't hurt her. Okay."

Winston shook his head.

"Look, I get it. We're just algae in a giant pond. But James, it's always been this way."

He stopped abruptly, throwing an arm out to block James from walking farther.

"What are you playing at? Testing my loyalty? Did Mark put you up to this?"

James hesitated; his gaze fixed on the darkness ahead.

"I'm not playing at anything. And no, I haven't spoken to Mark—geez, I wouldn't dare. The guy's a straight suit."

He glanced sideways at Winston. "I'm just saying… things feel a little uneven. Disproportionate. Maybe it's time for a—" he dragged out the word, waiting for his friend's reaction. "—rebellion."

Winston exhaled sharply, tossing his hands up before letting them drop to his sides.

"Yep. You're gonna get us killed. Treason. They're gonna charge us with treason and burn us on the altar of Hanwi."

They walked in silence another mile James humming as twigs snapped underfoot.

"You know a deaf man could hear you coming." Winston stated slightly agitated. James's attention was lost and he figured they might as well call it a night.

"I have an idea." James halted a few feet ahead, his gaze tilted skyward, eyes glimmering with that faraway look he always got when inspiration struck.

Winston exhaled sharply, rolling his eyes. *Not again.*

He scanned their surroundings, resisting the urge to groan. James had already shared enough, and Winston needed to find a way—any way—to shut this down before his friend got himself killed. If James kept pushing this reckless social justice crusade, they'd both suffer the consequences. As his scout partner, Winston was guilty by association, especially since he hadn't reported James the first time he'd heard this nonsense. Dread coiled in Winston's stomach. He almost didn't want to ask.

"An idea?" He sighed, already bracing for the worst. "Do tell."

James spun on his heels, his expression alight with conviction.

"We talk to the Alpha. We take this to Caesar and make our concerns known."

* * *

"Another delay?" Caesar's gaze bore into the old man across from him, his expression carefully concealing the fury simmering beneath the surface.

"Yes, Caesar. Another delay. This time, a necessary one," Reynolds said, his fingers resting lightly on the head of his cane, the other hand limp in his lap.

Caesar exhaled slowly, reining in his impatience.

"I'm sure you have an explanation for this... delay?"

His voice remained measured, but the weight behind his words was unmistakable. Caesar continued.

"Before you begin, understand this—I have reviewed our doctrine. Nowhere does it require a full moon for the ritual. A waning one will suffice."

He rose to his feet, his presence towering.

"With the High Table and the Council suspended, I have the authority to order the ceremony myself. But I want unity. I want to work with the Council and the other governing bodies, not against them." His sharp gaze swept across the room. "These meetings are a courtesy, gentlemen. A mere formality." He stated his disgust laced into each word spoken.

Reynolds remained silent, his eyes downcast as he sifted through centuries of doctrine both domestic and foreign, the rules that had governed the anointing of alphas for generations. Another pair of eyes bore into him—Elijah's.

"We share your desire for cooperation," Reynolds stated, his voice even. "We are willing to work with you, but revoking our authority was a mistake. This isn't just about timing, Caesar." He adjusted his grip on his cane. "All prominent members must be present. Not just your wife and sister—several key alphas must bear witness. You need to be officially recognized before you can engage in any diplomatic pursuits."

Caesar's patience frayed.

"And where is this written? What decree demands it?" His jaw tensed. "I have combed through every doctrine and found nothing."

Things should have been moving forward by now. Damien had upheld his end of the deal, deploying scouts stateside. Caesar was confident they'd have better luck finding Armand than his own.

Yet, for every piece that fell into place, something else veered off course.

His sister had been avoiding him for over a week. Evelyn, too, was... different. Withdrawn. Restless. He had caught her watching him more than once, her gaze distant, unreadable. She barely slept. It wasn't just the pregnancy. It was something else. Something deeper.

And he didn't like it.

The ceremonial delay only worsened the situation. Without official recognition, Caesar couldn't sign the Decree of the Federation. The longer he remained sidelined, the more fragile this venture became—it was at risk of collapsing before it even began.

"Not everything is written in books, young Caesar." Elijah leaned forward, his dark green eyes glinting with amusement. "Traditions aren't just ink on a page—they're upheld. Enforced. If necessary, violently." His smile deepened, wrinkles settling into the lines of his face. "Besides, you shouldn't be worrying about business. You should be on your honeymoon, enjoying your new wife."

Caesar's ground his teeth, pale lips curved into a forced grimace.

"I can enjoy my wife in the comfort of my home," he said coolly. "But I have more pressing matters—my brother, the Federation. These are things that need to be addressed."

William raised a hand, cutting him off.

"These are matters that cannot be discussed prior to official recognition."

Caesar's patience snapped.

"Then recognize me so we can get on with business!" His voice rang through the chamber as he rose to his feet. "A unification of the Covens across the globe will benefit us all. Think of the wealth, the influence we could wield. Gentlemen," he spread his arms, "it's time we stepped out of the shadows. Consolidated power will allow us to do just that."

William scoffed, shaking his head.

"There's no need to persuade us, Caesar." His voice was firm, unwavering. "I speak for us all when I say this Federation—this wolf version of the UN—has been discussed at length. And unanimously rejected. We want no part in it." He gestured to the men around the table. "You think stepping into the light will grant us power? It will paint targets on every wolf's back. It'll be the Dark Ages all over again."

A muscle twitched in Caesar's jaw as his fury surfaced. His olive complexion turned pallid, his pupil dilating with barely restrained rage.

But William didn't stop. He pressed on, his voice sharp as a blade.

"You misunderstand what it means to be an alpha, young Caesar. It's not a throne. You don't sit above us, barking orders, expecting blind obedience. It's cooperation. Give and take. There are privileges that come with the title you crave so desperately—but burdens, too." He leaned forward. "Your father understood that. Every man at this table understands that. Except you." William finished his gaze hard.

Caesar exhaled slowly, rising to his full height. His gaze swept across the room, cold and unyielding.

"You forget—my father isn't here." His voice was quiet, but the weight behind it filled the space. "I understand perfectly. It is you who lacks understanding."

"Speaking of your father," Charles interjected, his fingers laced together as he leaned forward. "It's improper to crown a new alpha while the former one hasn't been laid to rest. Especially when we don't have a confirmed cause of death."

Caesar's eye darkened.

"They should have been buried by now. I gave the order for the Crossing Over Ceremony to be performed, yet you keep delaying it—moving their bodies, withholding their rest." His voice sharpened. "You are the reason for this delay, Charles. And I have yet to figure out what game you're playing."

"Game?" Charles tilted his head, his expression unreadable. He leaned back in his chair, palms now flat on the table. "I'm not playing at anything, Caesar. I only want the truth. And I think everyone here—including you—wants that as well."

Caesar's jaw clenched. "I know the truth. You all forget I was there. I gave an eye." He lifted his hand, and pulled to the side the eye patch revealing the scarred skin over the eye socket.

Charles barely spared it a glance.

"Yes, but aren't you the least bit curious?" His tone was mild, almost conversational. "Your brother—your father's chosen successor—had everything. Power. Legacy. The world in the palm of his hand." His gaze lingered on Caesar. "So tell me… what reason would he have to murder the man that empowered him?"

A heavy silence thickened the air, pressing down on the room like a storm waiting to break.

Caesar's muscles coiled with restrained fury, his emerald eye burning. "Your point?" he ground out.

"My point is that until we have a reason—a real motive—I see no cause to bury them. Not just yet." Charles spread his hands. "The Coven remains stable. Business is uninterrupted. And I see no immediate threat on the horizon. At least… not until this matter is resolved."

"I second that, Charles," Elijah drawled as he rose from his chair. He smoothed the front of his suit with an easy smirk. "Gentlemen, I believe this meeting is over. There's a certain French woman in town who requires my attention."

Laughter rippled through the room as several others followed him out.

Caesar remained standing; his expression carved from stone. Only when the last of them had gone did Alan step to his side.

"Shall I bring the car around?"

Caesar exhaled through clenched teeth. If the Council refused to grant him power, he would take it by other means.

* * *

He slumped into the backseat, watching the trees blur past. Exhaustion weighed on him, pressing against his shoulders like an unseen force. He had given Alan the address and barely managed to crawl into the SUV, his body heavy with defeat.

Everything was supposed to fall into place once his father was gone. He hadn't expected his mother to eliminate him—let alone remove herself from the equation. His sigh was quiet but sharp, his gaze flicking from the roof of the SUV to the back of Alan's head before settling on the windshield. Their deaths meant nothing to him. No grief, no remorse. His only regret was that Armand hadn't joined them.

A dark shape loomed ahead, the shack appearing like a shadow against the landscape. He straightened, shifting to the edge of his seat.

Alan veered onto the overgrown patch of grass, his grip tightening on the wheel. A prickle ran down his spine. The energy surrounding the place was wrong. It was heavy, unsettling. A quick glance in the rear-view mirror confirmed he wasn't alone in his assessment. His boss felt it too. Dark hairs stood rigid along the man's forearms peeking beneath the cuffs of the button down.

"Sir, I don't think this is a good idea," Alan murmured, fingers still curled around the steering wheel. He hadn't even put the SUV in park.

"It's not your duty to think, Alan. Just obey."

"Yes, sir." The response came swiftly, clipped.

Caesar studied the shack's windows, expecting stillness—emptiness. Then, movement. A flutter of a curtain. Someone was inside.

Without hesitation, he pushed open the door. "Stay here," he ordered over his shoulder before stepping out.

The door slammed shut, and Alan shook. This didn't feel right and he reached for his phone, slipping it from the pocket of his blazer.

* * *

Reynolds excused himself from the table, his wife and grandchildren barely glancing his way before resuming their animated chatter.

"Yes?" His voice was low as he pressed the phone to his ear.

"I'm with Caesar. I'm not sure what this place is—some kind of shack. The energy here is… off."

"Do you recognize the location? Anything familiar?"

"Negative, sir. I'll drop a pin."

"Good. Watch him and keep me posted."

"Yes, sir."

Reynolds exhaled slowly, his grip tightening around the phone.

"Alan, remember—you are a good man. Loyal to the pack. Above all, loyal to the Coven. Don't let this weigh on you. Your reputation remains intact, and when this is over, you and your family will be greatly rewarded."

Alan was still hesitate with agreeing to spy on his boss but the offer was too good to pass up.

"Thank you, sir." Alan whispered looking around.

The call ended and the driver quickly shared his location before slipping the phone back into his pocket. He was loyal. Always had been. But Caesar's actions were not how an alpha behaved.

* * *

Reynolds opened the message, his pulse quickening as he read the address. He knew the place. He was aware who, or whether, to what it belonged. The Two Sisters—or rather, the one who existed in two forms within this realm. If they were part of Caesar's plan then he was playing a dangerous game. Breaking a promise to the sisters meant ruin. Death. A curse upon your bloodline.

He slipped the phone away and returned to the table, easing back into the warmth of his grandchildren's chatter unease clinging to him like a second skin.

* * *

Caesar was near the door when the stench of decay struck him like a fist. It wasn't overpowering enough to turn him back, but it curled in his gut, a slow, nauseating churn. He swallowed against the bile rising in his throat.

The rotted wood scraped against his knuckles as he rapped twice. The door creaked open, seemingly of its own accord. He exhaled sharply and stepped inside. Everything in him screamed to leave, but the vision pushed him forward. The larger goal. He had come too far to let doubt creep in now.

"Welcome."

The voice was hoarse yet laced with an unexpected power. He followed the sound, the warped floorboards groaning beneath his steps, shifting unevenly beneath his weight.

"Caesar, I knew you would come. What can I do for you?"

He halted at the small circular table, fighting the sneer threatening to twist his lips. It wasn't just the stench—his skin crawled, every sense bristling in protest. The room reeked of something old, something wrong.

"After some research, I discovered you're the only one who can give me what I desire."

A slow exhale. The figure across from him barely moved.

"I believe I know what you seek," she murmured. "This isn't the first time one of your kind has come. Here. To me. Another alpha."

"Sit."

The second voice was sharper, distinct from the first. The woman lifted a long, discolored nail and pointed to a chair behind him. It hadn't been there before. The back of his knees pressed against the seat, and he recoiled, his focus shifting to the shadowed corner where the unseen speaker lurked.

The hairs on his forearms stood on end despite the tailored weight of his suit. The woman at the table gestured to the chair again, her movement slow, reverent. Jaw tight, he lowered himself onto the worn wood. Forget dry cleaning—he'd have Alan burn the suit when they left.

Silence swallowed the room as he locked eyes with the woman. Her irises were clouded, unreadable, yet he knew she saw more than most.

"Surely, you came for more than to sit and stare at my sister."

The voice slithered from the shadows. The woman in the corner shifted, sliding toward the edge of her seat until the dim light revealed her. She was just as grotesque as the one across from him—leathery skin stretched tight over angular bones, milky eyes glistening with a mischievousness that gave him pause.

Caesar inhaled slow. Deep. His lungs burned from the stale air. He saw no point in prolonging this. The drive back to Birmingham would be long enough without unnecessary delays.

Leaning over the table, he whispered, "Are there ways to enhance my power?"

The witch mirrored his movement, her lips peeling into a grin. The wood groaned beneath her weight, and for a fleeting moment, darkened canines flashed behind cracked lips.

"Yes. Of course. I can give you all that you desire." Her voice curled around him like smoke, thick and cloying. "Even the things you don't yet know you desire. But… what are you willing to give for this power?"

"Money. I have plenty of it." His gaze flicked over the patchy walls, the water-stained ceiling, the air thick with damp rot. "Name an amount. You two could use it."

The last part was muttered under his breath, barely audible, as he swallowed down the sneer threatening to surface.

Laughter erupted from her, the sound carrying a gust of foul air that curled around him, rancid and thick. His fingers dug into the edge of the table, fighting the instinct to recoil.

"Money is not what we seek," she rasped. "Money is easy to acquire. Your wife is due to give birth—" she reached forward, skeletal fingers clamping around his wrist, her lids fluttering shut "—in a little less than a week."

His breath caught. The room felt smaller, the air heavier. He already knew where this was headed.

"I see twins. Boys"

"I suppose," he murmured. He hadn't wanted to know the sex—told Evelyn he didn't care—but deep down, he had his hopes. And boys were not it.

"I, we," she gestured toward the blind woman in the corner, "want one."

The older woman rose. Her dress slid down, revealing a bony, emaciated shoulder, yet when she spoke, her voice rang clear.

"It must be the stronger of the two."

Caesar's expression darkened.

"Why?" His voice was quieter now, edged with calculation. "Is there something else you want? My sister?" He gestured absently, his gaze sweeping over the shack. "She's still a virgin—you could train her."

"If you have to question the price, then you cannot afford it," the witch said, her voice dry as brittle leaves. "It's no matter if you are unwilling to pay."

"Wait!" Caesar lifted a hand. "I never said I was unwilling—just curious. What do you want with a child? Especially out here."

His desire to conquer outweighed whatever faint attachment he had to his unborn offspring. He and Evelyn were young and fertile. There would be more children.

Scenarios played through his mind. If they were twins, giving one away could be beneficial for the other. He would, of course, keep the stronger of the two as his heir. But then another thought took root—he could agree to the deal, take what he needed, and when the time came, simply eliminate them. A choice was made.

"Yes," he said, voice smooth, calculated. "I accept your terms. When do you need him?"

Dark, decayed teeth gleamed in the flickering candlelight as the witch smiled.

"When the child is five. By then, the stronger of the two will reveal himself. That is the one we require."

"A full-blooded wolf, at last," a voice murmured from the shadows.

"When can we do the ceremony?" Caesar asked.

Darkened teeth seemed to shimmer, caught in the dim glow.

"Tonight, dear. Tonight."

The other woman spoke for only the third time that evening, her sudden closeness making Caesar stiffen. For a moment, his guard slipped, fear flickering in his eye. He wanted to recoil in disgust. The unease coiling in his stomach far outweighed the fleeting rush of triumph in his chest. Madeline and Maggie rose in unison. Madeline extended a hand.

Caesar hesitated, staring down at the dry, calloused palm, willing himself not to react. When he took it, he was momentarily surprised by its unexpected softness.

"This way, Caesar," she murmured. "We have everything we need to begin."

6

Restoration

T he two sisters flanked him at the front door, standing on either side as he stared at it.

"I thought we were about to begin," he said, shifting his gaze from Madeline to the hollowed, shadowed face of Maggie. His lip curled in disgust before he forced it back down. The energy in the shack buzzed pressing against his skin. Sweat clung to his back, his shirt damp and sticking uncomfortably.

"We are," Madeline murmured, lifting a hand to grasp his chin. She whistled softly, guiding his face toward her. "But first, you need to get rid of him."

She pointed toward the window. Outside, Alan stood by the SUV, arms crossed, his posture tense.

"I'll need him to drive me back," Caesar said.

Maggie chuckled, the sound a brittle rasp as she leaned close, her breath ghosting over his ear.

"What we're about to give you, you won't need to be driven back."

Her cracked lips brushed his skin in a mockery of a kiss, and he shuddered. Goosebumps prickled his arms as the dry scrape of her mouth lingered against his pinna. A cold, crawling sensation slithered over him. He needed a bath. But he forced himself to stand still until they decided to release him.

"Go," they commanded, their voices blending into a single, eerie harmony.

He moved slowly, careful not to seem too eager to leave their presence. Alan straightened as Caesar approached, one hand already reaching for the SUV's door handle.

"I need you to leave," Caesar ordered.

Alan hesitated, glancing past his alpha toward the open door of the shack.

"Sir," he said, uncertainty flickering in his eyes.

Caesar sighed, his patience thinning.

"Don't question me. I'll be fine. Go. Now."

The sharp command left no room for argument. Alan gave a curt nod, slid into the driver's seat, and pulled away, the SUV kicking up dust as it rolled down the dirt road. Half a mile out, he eased the vehicle to a stop and cut the engine.

The unease had been gnawing at him since they arrived, but now it was clawing at his gut. Alan checked his watch. He'd give it twenty minutes. Then he was going back. He needed to see for himself what his alpha was doing. Then he'd report to Reynolds.

* * *

Caesar watched as the sleek black metal disappeared around the bend, swallowed by the dense tree line. The shift in the air was immediate. The sky had been bright and cloudless near the cabin when he arrived, but now, the light dimmed, the atmosphere thickening with something unseen yet tangible.

He took note of the sudden darkness, then turned back to the sisters. Maggie and Madeline faced each other, bowing low in perfect unison before righting themselves and turning toward him. Without a word, they extended their hands. He hesitated only for a moment before taking them, inhaling deeply as his fingers brushed their cold skin. They led him through the house, past the room where they had first met. Only now, it was bare.

He turned in a slow circle, taking in its stark transformation. The once-cluttered space was now cleared, illuminated solely by the flickering glow of countless candles. Their dim, wavering light cast shifting shadows, bathing the room in an eerie, almost familiar warmth. He frowned.

He had seen this before. Lived this before.

"Stand there."

The sisters pointed to the center of a large square marked on the wooden floor. He obeyed, his gaze flicking to them as they approached. Their tattered rags were gone. In their place, pristine robes shrouded their forms, hoods drawn low over their faces. Only their bare forearms were exposed, the pale, taut flesh stark against the dim candlelight.

"Remove your clothes."

The command was soft, but absolute. Caesar slowly unbuttoned his blazer, sliding it from his shoulders.

"All of them."

Their voices had changed—where once they had been haggard and cracked, they were now silken, each syllable rolling over him like a caress. The shift in their tone sent a pulse of anticipation skittering down his spine.

He wet his lips, stripping off his shirt. The fine fabric leaving whispers against his skin as he let it fall. His shoes followed, then his trousers, and finally, his briefs. He kicked the garments out of the marked square, the cool air licking his bare skin.

The sisters moved in tandem, parting. One stepped before him, the other behind.

Then they raised their hands. A single, deafening clap shattered the silence, and the dim light overhead extinguished, leaving only the flickering glow of the candles. From behind, an incantation coiled through the air, the words indecipherable. Hypnotic.

In front, a different voice—softer, melodic—whispered through the space, lulling him forward. He gasped as the woman before him lowered her hood. She was young. Beautiful.

Her robe slipped from her shoulders, pooling at her feet. The chanting behind him rose in pitch, a relentless vibration that thrummed through his skull, rattling his bones. His breath hitched. His pulse quickened. And as she stepped toward him, his body responded. He shut his eye, his mind latching onto the image of Evelyn.

Her soft curves. The warmth of her touch. The way she looked at him—like he was the center of her world. He didn't want to betray her. The thought alone sent a shock through his body. The arousal that had stirred within him faded, leaving him cold. Ashamed. His frame went rigid as he felt a foreign body press against him, her breath hot against his ear. Then—a pull. Fingers ghosting over his cheek, prying at the edge of his eye patch. He grabbed her wrist, his grip tight.

"No," he hissed.

A whisper danced over his lips, soft yet insistent.

"See."

The patch was gone. A sharp inhale left him as he blinked, his mind refusing to accept what his eyes told him. Both of them. He could see. His vision, whole once more, locked onto the woman before him. She held his gaze, unwavering, her fingers trailing between them. Then she reached down. Caesar jolted as her hand wrapped around him.

"No. Not like this."

He moved to stop her, but before he could, the chanting ceased.

Warmth enveloped him from behind. Another strange body. The second sister pressed against his back, firm breasts and hard nipples grazing his skin. He shuddered as her arms coiled around his torso, one hand sliding over his chest. A chuckle rumbled near his ear.

"Maybe this will help, sister."

She spun him effortlessly, turning him to face—Evelyn. His breath left him in a rush. She was there. In front of him. The same deep brown eyes he had memorized. The same full lips, slightly parted, the promise of something familiar lingering on them.

"Caesar."

His name left her lips in a sultry whisper, the very tone she always used when she wanted to pull him under her spell. His mind screamed it wasn't real. That this was trickery, an illusion. Magic at its darkest. But his body—his traitorous body—fell for it. She was his anchor. His partner. The woman who stood beside him as he clawed his way to power. When she kissed him, he surrendered.

His hands roamed over the dark flesh pressed against him, gripping, claiming. A low laugh vibrated against his mouth, but he barely noticed. He was lost. Drowning. Madeline watched, a smirk playing at her lips as Maggie guided Caesar deeper into the embrace. Then, without pause, she lifted her hands high above her head. The curved blade gleamed in the candlelight.

With precise, practiced ease, she dragged the tip down the center of her palm, splitting flesh. Dark, viscous blood seeped from the wound. It oozed thickly, not red, but black. Like tar. Rot. Death. She brought her hand to her face, studying the corrupted liquid as it pulsed from her skin. Then she stepped forward, chanting. Maggie broke the kiss, spinning Caesar to face Madeline. It was time.

"Drink, my love," Maggie whispered against his ear, her breath ghosting across his sensitive skin.

The voice. So much like Evelyn's. For a moment, he forgot. Forgot where he was. Forgot what was real.

"Drink," she murmured again.

His eyes fluttered open—and it wasn't Maggie standing before him anymore.

Hera.

She smiled at him. It was the kind of smile that had always been just out of reach, soft and inviting, the way he had only ever seen her look at Armand. Never at him. Never like this.

"Drink, brother."

Her voice dripped with something he thought her incapable of —seduction. Her outstretched palm, slick with blood, hovered between them. Caesar stared, transfixed.

Had she ever looked at him like this? Even as children, had she ever gazed at him with such warmth?

He couldn't recall. His body moved before his mind could catch up, instinct overriding thought. Fingers tightened around her delicate wrist, pulling her closer. The scent of iron filled his nostrils, rich and cloying, but he didn't recoil.

He didn't hesitate as lips parted and he drank. Warm, thick liquid coated his tongue, sweeter than it should have been. Like honey melted into blood. Hera gasped, her breath hitching, a small sigh slipping past her lips. The sound sent a ripple through him, and he hummed against her palm. *How long had he been drinking?*

He pulled away suddenly, gasping for air. The stickiness clung to his lips, his tongue, his throat. It lingered like warm sugar, dissolving into his senses. Then—warmth.

A body against his back, lips pressing soft, wet kisses down the length of his spine. Lower. Over the curve of his buttocks. Then back up, slow and deliberate, before stopping at his shoulder. Still, he hadn't let go of Hera. She stepped closer, her free hand sliding down, claiming him. Caesar sucked in a sharp breath, his muscles tensing beneath her touch.

"It's okay, brother," she whispered, her lips hovering near his own. "You've wanted this for a long time. I can tell."

The words slithered into his mind, twisting through the tangled threads of what he knew was wrong—and what his body wanted. A second presence appeared at his side. Evelyn. He turned his head, staring into the deep brown eyes that owned him. His grip on Hera's wrist loosened as his free hand reached for her. The Evelyn who had always known him.

He crashed his lips against hers, drowning in the familiar taste of her mouth. The softness. The rightness. And yet—when he pulled away—his gaze landed back on Hera. The forbidden. This wasn't real. This Hera wasn't real.

But if he indulged…

If he gave in…

Would it really matter?

Caesar hummed against her lips, the vibration passing between them like a broken promise. Hot kisses were exchanged, hands exploring, grasping, laying claim. Their touches mirrored each other, guiding him downward until he lay on his back. Above him, they knelt. One on either side.

"Which one of us should go first?"

Two voices, one sound. The Evelyn-like figure reached out, brushing a stray hair from Hera's face, her touch almost reverent.

"He's waited so long for you," she murmured, her gaze never leaving him. "You go first."

Caesar swallowed hard, his throat tight, his cock aching. The sisters noticed.

"I believe you're right." Hera's voice barely a breathy whisper.

Slowly, she straddled him. Heat. Softness. Skin against skin. His stomach tightened as he felt her bare sex press against his lower abdomen.

"She's still a virgin," Maggie purred in his ear. "You have to guide her, my love."

His breath came faster. His heart pounding. He placed his hands on her waist, lifting her slightly, positioning her over his length. Their eyes locked—dark green swallowing his own.

"Grab me."

The command wavered, uncertainty creeping in. Maggie chuckled, her breath hot against his ear.

"You can do better than that, love. What do you want her to grab?"

Her lips brushed his jaw, her voice dropping into something honeyed and dark.

"Tell her."

The hesitation bled from him.

"Grab my dick."

His voice was stronger. Certain. Hera's lips parted as she timidly reached down, her small fingers wrapping around him.

"Guide me in."

She nodded, obeying – a mischievous glint in her eyes. A shudder ran through him as he slowly pulled her down, sinking into a tight, unfamiliar heat. Both of them sighed. His head fell back, eyes rolling shut.

Pleasure.

Guilt.

Two forces—colliding, entwining, battling. But he pushed the shame aside, shoved it into some dark corner of himself where it could fester and die. Pleasure won. He surrendered to them. The power, the darkness, the fantasy.

* * *

Enough. Alan had waited too long. The forty-five minutes moved like a slow, dripping faucet. He glanced down at his cell, checking for any messages. There were no new updates. No orders. Just a read receipt from Reynolds—a silent acknowledgment. Nothing more.

Stripping off his clothes in the front seat, he shifted, his muscles twisting and reshaping until fur replaced flesh. The moment the transformation completed; he launched through the window. The woods breathed around him.

Danger and the feel of death pressed against his coat; the fine hairs rose painfully in their follicles. The closer he crept to the house, the worse it became—a pulsing energy that hummed beneath his paws.

Instinct screamed at him to turn back. He ignored it. Keeping low, he moved through the underbrush, circling toward the back of the house. His sharp eyes scanned the structure, searching. Then he found it. A cracked, grimy window.

He stepped closer, pressing his snout against the glass. Had he been in human form, he would have gasped. Inside, his alpha lay on his back, writhing in some twisted mixture of pleasure and pain. Two women—replicas of his wife and sister—crawled over him, their tongues tracing patterns over blushed skin. Then Evelyn straddled him, her head falling back in ecstasy as the other woman watched her lips moving.

Alan stiffened as he planted his paw further into the earth. Impossible. Every nerve in his body screamed this wasn't real.

What manner of sorcery was this?

He tore himself away from the window, heart hammering, bile rising in his throat. He had seen enough. With quick, practiced movements, he sprinted back to the SUV. Once inside, he yanked on his clothes, shaking fingers fumbling with the buttons of his vest. He fired off a text to Reynolds.

Urgent. We need to meet. TONIGHT. It's worse than you thought.

Only when the message was sent did he allow himself to breathe.

This place. This magic. He had never been this deep into the woods before. But he had heard the stories. Of those who lived in the shadows, preying on their kind. Creatures who bartered with blood. Of dark magic that craved the essence of a pureblood wolf, in exchange for the gifts it offered.

* * *

Caesar woke on the floor. For a moment, he lay still, disoriented. The air was heavy with the scent of sex and something earthy—damp wood, old stone. *How long had he been asleep?* Time felt… slippery. The sisters were gone. No trace of them remained.

As he sat up, his body thrummed with energy. He finally felt alive. He placed a hand on his stomach and froze.

Ceasar was clothed again. He traced his finger over his upper body and arms. Everything was covered and in order as if they'd never been disturbed. The house was exactly as it had been when he first arrived. The rough floorboard scratched at his bottom and the back of his thighs. He took in the shabby surroundings before standing. It had all been a trick. A hallucination.

But then—

His hand drifted to his face. The second his fingers brushed the smooth, unbroken skin, his breath hitched. There were no scars. The hollowness was now filled out, round. The dull ache he had grown accustomed was gone.

He had both eyes. The realization crashed into him, and a slow, delirious grin spread across his lips. Whatever else happened, whatever the price—this, at least, was real.

* * *

Alan sank into the leather seat, checking the time. Five and a half hours. Caesar had disappeared into that house, and not a single sound had come from within. Alan wasn't one to abandon his post, but after what he'd seen through that filthy window, every instinct screamed at him to leave. To drive. Most importantly—to forget. His fingers twitched on the wheel. He could still do it. Just start the engine, press the gas—a shape moved in the driver's side window.

Alan flinched, his hand flying to his weapon. He sighed in relief when a familiar face emerged from the darkness.

Caesar.

Alan exhaled sharply, reaching for the door handle.

"Alpha— my apologies. I would have come back to pick you up. You should have called." He tried to open the door, but it was immediately closed.

Alan applied more pressure but stopped when the extra effort proved to be in vain. The grip was too strong. Unnatural. He hesitated before looking up. Alan wasn't sure how he didn't realize before. He recoiled. His Alpha's ruined socket was restored, replaced with a second, gleaming iris. And the grin the man wore made him shiver in the Alabama heat.

Alan swallowed. "I'll take you back to the city, sir." His fingers tightened on the handle.

"No need." Caesar tilted his head, his voice smooth, amused. "I'll drive myself."

Alan stiffened. Something felt... off. This man, this thing, wasn't the same one he had driven into these woods.

"I insist," Alan murmured, every nerve on edge. He didn't know why, but he couldn't let Caesar go alone.

Caesar laughed.

The sound slithered over Alan's skin, cold and oily.

"No, Alan. Your job was to leave. Not to come back. And certainly—" his voice dropped to a near purr, "not to spy on me."

Alan's heart lurched. "Sir, I—"

The words died in his throat—along with his breath. Caesar's hand shot through the window, clamping around his neck. In one swift motion Alan was pulled through the window in a vain attempt to stop Caesar he grabbed his arm. He felt the man's strength as the muscles pulsated beneath the fabric.

Alan gasped, a wet, choking sound. His windpipe crunched in Caesar's grip—then tore free. A garbled wheeze escaped him before his body collapsed onto the gravel in a heap. Caesar counted the twitching, amused. Death had come later than expected for his driver. He exhaled slowly, dropping the ruined flesh beside him. He crouched, plucked Alan's phone from his pocket, and held it over the man's face. The screen unlocked with a blink.

Perfect.

With a flick of his finger, he changed the password, slipping the phone into his coat. The messages could wait. Right now, his body burned. His blood sang. Power thrummed through his veins. He felt alive, insatiable. His hunger stretched beyond the kill. The night was young. Sliding into the driver's seat, Caesar flipped down the sun visor, studying his reflection. His gaze locked onto his restored eye.

He grinned. It was perfect. They had done it. Slamming the visor shut, he gripped the wheel, floored the gas, and tore out of the woods.

7

Re-Birth and Birth

A lan's phone rested on the seat beside him, the screen aglow. Caesar had sent a simple message to Reynolds—"Done. Heading back."

Nothing more. The tires screeched as he rounded a steep curve, he pressed the pedal to the floor. Reckless? Maybe. But he felt invincible. His own phone buzzed in his pocket. He ignored it. It buzzed again. His jaw clenched.

He had made it clear he wasn't to be disturbed. *Who dared?* A third time. Growling, he yanked the phone free and took the call. His voice dripped with venom.

"Speak!" Spittle flecked the wheel.

A hesitant voice crackled on the line.

"Sir—my apologies for the disturbance."

A pause. Too long.

"Get on with it!" Caesar snapped, yanking the phone away from his ear. Heat burned behind his eyes, rage curling in his gut. If this was anything but urgent, someone was losing their head—

"It's your wife, sir. She's in labor."

The words struck him like a fist to the ribs.

Labor? Now?

His mind blanked. He wasn't ready. Nothing was ready. The SUV lurched as his foot eased off the gas.

"Sir?" The voice repeated the words. Twice.

Caesar swallowed; his mouth suddenly dry. "Where is she?" His voice barely more than a whisper.

"At home. The midwife is with her."

Home. The place he had avoided. His fingers tightened on the wheel. Power thrummed through his veins. His blood demanded more. He had just been **reborn—**how could he be expected to walk back into that house as the same man?

He inhaled sharply. "Stay with her. I'm on my way."

Silence hung on the line between them. The young caller afraid to disconnect before he had confirmation Caesar disconnected the call.

"…Yes, sir."

Caesar stared ahead. His thoughts churned. His instincts warred. He didn't respond. With a sharp flick, he ended the call and tossed the phone into the backseat, cutting himself off from any further interruptions.

The SUV roared as he merged onto the freeway, speedometer climbing, tires gripping the asphalt like a predator chasing prey. He was running—he just didn't know where. But home? That was the last place he wanted to be. Not now. Not with the boys coming.

* * *

Evelyn fought to stay on her feet, but the pain clawing through her body made it impossible. She gripped the bedpost, knuckles ashen, legs trembling. The woman her brother had sent stood in the corner, unreadable, while the others rushed frantically around her. She didn't speak much but she did give her name. Zinhle.

The men had excused themselves after the first labor pain. It was the only confirmation needed and they exited the room claiming this was woman's work. Evelyn barely registered the news that several councilmen had arrived and had previously been in her presence. *Why were they here?* The only person she needed—the only one she wanted—was her husband.

And he wasn't there.

Lately, she didn't know where he went or what secrets he carried. He was more of a closed book now than when they first met. A fresh contraction seized her, fire ripping through her body. "Ahhh—" Her breath hitched as she doubled over.

"Madame, you must lie down," a young woman urged, placing a hand on her shoulder. Evelyn swatted it away, but the sharp movement only worsened the pain. She gasped, grimacing.

"Madame, lie down."

This time, an older woman stepped forward, shoving the younger one aside. She had the air of someone who had done this a hundred times and wasn't about to coddle her. Unlike the other woman, she didn't try to touch her.

"NO!" Evelyn hissed as another pain crashed into her. Something felt wrong. This was her first time, but even she knew this wasn't how it should be. The older woman planted both hands on her hips, expression unimpressed.

"What is all this fuss? You are not the first wolf woman to have a child, and you won't be the last." Her tone was sharp, no-nonsense. Under different circumstances, Evelyn might have liked her—another gift from her brother.

"Something is wrong," she managed, chest rising and falling too fast. "It's too soon—two weeks. Two weeks."

The words barely left her lips before her legs gave way. She braced for the hard slam of the floor, but strong arms caught her. Another pair joined in, lifting her onto the bed.

"Grab my bag. It's time," the older woman called to someone beyond Evelyn's line of sight.

The silent woman in the corner hadn't moved, her expression remained fixed. Unreadable. But Evelyn couldn't focus on the mystery woman—not when another contraction ripped through her, stealing her breath, forcing her body to curl inward. Hands held her down, keeping her from breaking under the pain.

The old African woman lingered in Evelyn's peripheral vision until, suddenly, hers was the only face that filled her world.

"Something unnatural is at work here," she murmured, leaning close, her breath warm against Evelyn's cheek. A rustling sound came from her bag. "But don't worry," she continued, voice steady, assured.

"We will bring you out on the right side of the darkness. The light will always win."

Evelyn barely had time to process the words before a new sensation overtook her—cold steel against the tight stretch of her belly. Her body jolted, but instead of pain, relief seeped into her bones, the clawing agony in her side easing.

But the sudden shift left her dizzy. She slumped against the pillows, her limbs heavy, her mind drifting. The pull of unconsciousness was intoxicating, seductive, luring her into darkness.

No.

She fought it, forcing her eyes to stay open even as they burned with dryness. She refused to fade. When she finally blinked, the movement felt sluggish, like she was swimming through molasses.

A soft whisper ghosted against her ear. "Push."

She obeyed, gripping the hands offered to her and bearing down with everything she had left. The strain sent a ringing through her ears, muting all other sounds—except one. The elder's whisper. It was urgent, insistent.

"Push."

Then—

"Ahh, the first one is out. A boy."

A sharp cry pierced the room, and Evelyn's body sagged. It was over. Or so she thought.

"Again! Push!"

The softness vanished, replaced by a command that cracked like a whip. A voice—deeper, rougher—shouted something. A man's voice. Caesar? She clenched her teeth, tightened her grip on the hands in hers, and pushed. A guttural scream tore from her throat as she felt something break free. Then silence. Then another cry.

Her grip slipped as her body gave out. The second wail joined the first, harmonizing in a song of life. Evelyn stared at the ceiling, her breath shaky, her heart thundering, but a wave of gratitude washed over her.

"It's done now, my child."

The words were as sweet as the cries of her newborns. It was officially over.

* * *

Caesar had hoped to arrive when it was over—after the ordeal had passed, once the children had made entry into their world, after the nanny stepped in to carry the weight he feared to bear.

He lingered outside, his breath uneven, hands curled into fists at his sides. The doorman's hand rested on the knob of his childhood home— the official residence of the Alpha. From within, his sharp hearing caught a single word.

Boys.

His pulse stuttered. The witches had been right. A shudder coursed through him, but not from fear. He had wanted them to be wrong, to give him an escape from the debt he now owed. But with every scream that tore from Evelyn's throat, a different reaction clawed at him. Her pain should have repulsed him—sickened him—but instead, it coiled around his spine, dark and insidious, feeding something he didn't want to name.

He swallowed hard, forcing himself still as he felt his erection press agaisnt his trouser. This terrified him the most. He had never been one to derive pleasure from suffering. But this? He could get used to this. When the screams finally dulled, he exhaled sharply, giving the doorman a curt nod. The man returned the motion and pushed the door open.

"Congratulations, Alpha."

A young woman he recognized as Sabrina—dipped her head, her voice tinged with excitement.

"Twins. Boys."

He sidestepped her without acknowledgment, inhaling deeply. Although faint, the scent hit him before he could brace for it—thick, warm, metallic. Before he could process it, a familiar figure stepped from the shadows.

"Congratulations, Caesar."

Reynolds.

A glass of cognac dangled from his hand, the amber liquid swirling lazily as he studied Caesar with sharp, searching eyes. His gaze flickered between Caesar's left and right eye, confusion knitting his brow. The two men stared each other down. Reynolds sensed it—that something in Caesar had changed. He couldn't quite place it, but it was there.

"Your eye?" He lifted his glass in a subtle gesture. Caesar's lips twitched. He spread his arms wide, an almost manic gleam in his gaze.

"I've been renewed," he said, his voice smooth, assured. "I'm back—better than before."

Reynolds' eyes narrowed. Caesar only grimaced. Plans to deal with the old fool would have to wait until later that evening.

"I must be going. As you know, when the children of a soon-to-be Alpha are born, we make it a point to bear witness and sense they are here and healthy there is no need for us to remain. We'll give you your privacy."

Reynolds set his glass down on a nearby table and turned to leave. As he passed Caesar, his hand instinctively came to rest on the man's shoulder—but the moment his palm met fabric, he recoiled. Something slithered beneath Caesar's skin, an energy both eerily familiar and out of place.

Reynolds' gaze snapped to Caesar's. It was sharp, knowing. There was a silent exchange between them. Something would need to do done. If his suspicions were correct, they were at Caesar's mercy. Unless someone was willing to do what had been done before.

The old man inclined his head in a subtle farewell and strode toward the front door. His pulse hammered in his ears. This was becoming eerily like before. Pulling his cell from his breast pocket, Reynolds scrolled through his contacts. His call went unanswered. Jaw tightening, he tapped out a text to Alan.

Meanwhile, Caesar remained still, eyes now closed, listening.

The house was alive with chatter, voices bleeding through the walls despite the soundproofing. He could hear everything. A smirk ghosted his lips. Then, a sound cut through it all. His children's cries. The smirk faded. His shoulders squared. He stepped around the corner, and at once, the room fell silent.

Council members turned toward him, some rising to their feet, their gazes sweeping over him—his stance, his face. Their confusion was palpable. And for some, so was the fear. Caesar smiled. This would be too easy. He had never felt this powerful in all his life.

"Gentlemen," he said smoothly, "good evening."

The response was hesitant, almost a chorus—uncertainty woven into every word.

"Congratulations, Caesar. You should be proud," Pierce said from his seat.

"I am. Thank you." Caesar inclined his head, then straightened. "And while I have you all here, we have business to discuss."

He let the weight of his words settle before continuing.

"With the birth of my sons, finding my brother is imperative. Your efforts have been inadequate."

"Caesar—" Pierce started, only to be cut off as Caesar lifted a hand.

"Alpha. I am your Alpha and will be addressed as such."

Pierce leaned back, discomfort flickering across his face. Still, he pressed on.

"Alpha, we have scouts searching across the state. They're looking for your brother and his fiancée, but every lead has hit a dead end. There's been no chatter of him attempting to reclaim anything. Aside from the alleged crime of murder, he poses no threat."

Caesar stepped forward. The air in the room thickened, his presence expanding, raw power rolling off him in waves. The gathered men felt it—he made sure of it.

"Kings fall because they dismiss a so-called 'benign' threat," he said smoothly. "My brother would not be a threat if he presented himself as one. But I know him. He waits, growing stronger in the process."

Several men shifted, preparing to speak, but Caesar silenced them with a flick of his hand.

"The Rite of Selene. No more delays. I want the ceremony scheduled immediately. Understood?"

A murmur of agreement rippled through the room, some nodding, others whispering their compliance.

"Good." He exhaled, as though satisfied. "We will finalize the details in the morning. For now, gentlemen, I bid you good night."

The council members rose, some downing their drinks in one swift motion before following the line of aged men toward the exit.

Only when the last of them had left did Caesar allow himself to breathe. Finally, things were falling into place. He turned toward the stairs, ascending slowly, deliberately. Each step dragged, the incline feeling steeper than it was. He wasn't ready to face what lay beyond that door. Twin boys. Yet all he could think about was him and his brother.

8

Out with the Old

H e placed a hand on the doorknob, steadying his nerves before stepping inside. The others in the room faded into the background as his focus locked onto her. Evelyn looked exhausted, yet her smile was wide, radiant. Beautiful. Caesar couldn't help but return it with one of his own.

Beside her, the younger woman lowered her gaze in silent acknowledgment of his authority. Across the room, the tall African woman remained unmoving, her stare fixed straight ahead. She neither spoke nor acknowledged him. Interesting.

He made a mental note to uncover the purpose of the woman's presence. He didn't like last minute additions to the staff. If she was a spy or an obstacle, she would be dealt with accordingly. Sensing their cue, the women swiftly excused themselves, leaving the new parents alone. Zinhle lingered shifting her gaze to Evelyn.

"Go, please," Evelyn whispered sharply, nodding toward the door. The woman obeyed leaving silently.

Only when they were alone did Caesar speak. If Evelyn noticed the change she didn't acknowledge it.

"What is her purpose?"

The curiosity of the unfamiliar woman momentarily outweighed his unease. He placed a careful hand on one of the twin's heads, the warmth of new life grounding him.

"I don't know," Evelyn admitted, her voice tinged with thought. "I assumed my brother sent her to assist with the birth, but that was the other woman. The stern, harsh looking one."

She paused, glancing toward the door.

"But her? She doesn't cook; she doesn't clean, and it's probably my fault I haven't given her any real tasks, but she doesn't seem inclined to take any on, either."

"Hmm." He didn't take his eyes off her, "don't worry about her for now."

She exhaled heavily, fatigue weighing down on her.

"Does this have to be discussed now?" Her gaze softened. "Your sons," she murmured, offering them to him. "Hold them."

He stiffened. His body resisted the motion, but Evelyn was patient as she carefully transferred the small bundles into his arms. Caesar cradled them tightly. They stirred, reacting to his warmth, his heartbeat. His resolve wavered. They could feel him. For a fleeting moment, the war brewing inside him quieted. But reality lingered just beneath the surface. One day, he would have to give one of them away.

That fate was years away—the old hags could be dead by then—but he knew. One day, they would come.

"They came early." Evelyn's voice was tinged with lingering disbelief. "It all happened so fast. This morning, I was fine—thinking we had at least another two weeks. Then, out of nowhere, I was in labor."

Caesar's jaw tightened. "When did the contractions start?" he murmured, keeping his gaze fixed downward.

He was beginning to see the connection—their birth and what happened at the shack.

Evelyn tilted her head, thinking.

"I'd say around six-thirty, maybe a little after. Why?"

His fingers twitched against the soft blanket, but he didn't answer. Instead, he asked, "Who's the oldest?"

If she noticed his abrupt deflection, she didn't show it. "The one on your left. Three minutes apart." She giggled, sinking into the pillows.

As if sensing that he was being talked about, the newborn yawned, his tiny chest expanding before settling back down. Caesar's chest ached, unfamiliar warmth pressing against the hatred he carried for his own father over the years. He wondered if they would inherit the same.

"What should we call them?" he asked.

"I don't know. I never picked anything out." She glanced at him. "Why don't you name one, and I'll name the other?"

Before he could respond, a soft knock broke the moment. The door creaked open, and Hera peeked inside, grinning like a child sneaking into a forbidden room.

"Can I come in?" she asked, already stepping forward and shutting the door behind her.

Caesar rolled his eyes. "I thought I told you I never wanted to see your face again."

Hera stopped short of the bed, arms crossed over her chest.

"I'm here for Evelyn and the babies," she shot back. "You can go back to hating me in the morning." She uncrossed her arms and plopped down beside her sister-in-law, completely unbothered.

"I don't hate you," he muttered.

"Sure," she quipped, unconvinced. Turning her attention away from him, she wrapped Evelyn in a warm hug.

"Caesar, be nice," Evelyn chided gently. "She just wants to see the twins."

"Fine." He relented, handing one of the boys to Evelyn and the other to Hera.

As he stepped back, he watched them—Evelyn, Hera, the twins. His family. He would do anything for them.

The phone vibrated in his pocket. His gaze flicked down. Reynolds.

* * *

Reynolds had served under two alphas in his long life. He had seen the days of lawlessness—when there was no order, only chaos. He would not go back. And he wouldn't stand idle while the Coven headed down that path again.

Maximillian's reckless youth had nearly destroyed the Coven before it had even found its footing. Reynolds refused to be a bystander a second time. If spying on Caesar kept them from spiraling into anarchy, then so be it. He would do what was necessary.

The hour was near, and still—no sign of the driver. He quickly sent a text, hoping the young man had managed to slip away from his boss unnoticed. A moment later, his phone buzzed. Confirmation. The young man was on his way. Reynolds smiled.

"Terry?"

"Yes, sir." The driver met his gaze in the rearview mirror.

"I'm going to step out, take a short walk beyond that tree line." He gestured ahead. "I'm meeting someone. Wait for me here. Give us about thirty minutes."

"Yes, sir."

Terry returned his attention to the book in his lap, indifferent. The pay wasn't good enough for him to care beyond basic obedience. Reynolds stepped out, the chill of the night brushing against his skin as he made his way toward the thicket. The journey wasn't long, but as he ventured deeper, the darkness thickened, swallowing the world behind him. The forest hummed with the undercurrent of life. The sounds wrapped around him like an old melody. He breathed deep; he could hear everything.

He made a mental note to bring Anna here again. It had been too long since they'd wandered the woods together. A rustling up ahead. Reynolds stopped cold. That wasn't Alan. His suspicions were confirmed when a shadow moved through the underbrush. Caesar. By the time he stepped into the clearing, the shift had completed. Reynolds swallowed hard, his gaze darting around. His driver was too far to be of any help, and he knew—this was the end.

There was no way he would make it out alive. At least... maybe he could get some answers before it was over.

"Expecting someone else?" Caesar's voice was rough, edged with amusement.

Reynolds tightened his grip on the head of his cane. "Where's your driver, Alan? You took him with you when you went to the Two Sisters to become this." He gestured toward him with a slight tilt of his head.

"What's left of him is scattered across some backwoods road that escapes me at the moment." Caesar's lips curled into a smirk. "I'm reborn, Reynolds."

"You call this rebirth?" Reynolds scoffed. "More like selling your soul to the devil."

Caesar chuckled, his Adam's apple bobbing as he laughed.

"Huh. You people don't understand power. Change. Vision. You, along with those other dullards, know nothing."

"I'm afraid it's you who's in the dark, Caesar." The older man shook his head, his gaze briefly falling to the ground before he looked back up, locking eyes with the younger man. "Your father always had concerns about you."

Caesar froze. The gruesome grin faded, replaced by something more guarded. He swallowed.

His father had concerns.

"Well," Caesar drawled, masking his curiosity behind indifference, "do tell."

Reynolds chuckled to himself. Too easy. The boy was fearless, but a man without fear could be easily baited.

"There are certain qualities you lack," Reynolds said, leveling his voice. "No respect. No regard for tradition. When you don't get your way, you throw tantrums and bully those around you." He sighed. "We don't trust you. And I assure you, it's nothing personal."

He tapped his cane into the dirt for emphasis. "Many didn't like your father either—but we respected him. He was a leader. A man we were proud to call Alpha."

Caesar scoffed.

"Please. Given what my father did, I don't think you'd be proud to call him anything."

"Ah," Reynolds tilted his head. "Now, you do tell."

Caesar's smirk returned, slow and deliberate.

"Your former Alpha—Samuel. My father, along with Charles, poisoned him." He let the words hang before finishing, "And then they murdered him."

Reynolds didn't so much as blink. Instead, he waved a dismissive hand.

"Smart man."

Caesar frowned.

"Samuel was very much like you," Reynolds continued, his tone almost amused. "Taking charge. Sticking his nose where it didn't belong, where it wasn't wanted. Your father saw a maniac and did what he thought needed to be done."

He shrugged. "I don't agree with the method—if what you say is true—but I do understand it."

He took a step back, his grin widening.

"Let me tell you something, dear boy. Samuel also went to the Two Sisters. They made him powerful. Enhanced the black magic he brought with him from Louisiana. Poisoning him was probably the only way to even the odds."

Reynolds chuckled, shaking his head. Caesar said nothing. For the first time that evening, he didn't feel quite as in control as he had before.

"Don't hate your father. Trust me—some of us have done far worse."

"Enough of this!" Caesar hissed, closing the distance between him and the older wolf in a flash. His muscles tensed with barely restrained fury.

"You had my driver spy on me. That can't be allowed."

"Before you rip out my throat – I suppose that's what's next – I must ask – what was their price? The Two Sisters?"

Caesar's jaw tightened at the question, but he exhaled sharply. It hardly mattered now—Reyonlds would be dead within the next minute.

"My son. The strongest of the two," he admitted, his voice laced with something akin to regret. His fingers curled around the collar of Reynolds' shirt, knuckles whitening.

The older man scoffed.

"I hardly think Evelyn would agree to such a thing."

Caesar shook his head.

"No. She doesn't know. Nor does she need to know. When she sees the benefit of all of this, she'll come around." His voice dropped to a whisper, uncertainty flickering in his eyes. But he clung to his conviction. Once their plans bore fruit, she would understand.

A dry chuckle escaped Reynolds.

"I highly doubt it. Keep chasing your delusions, and you will lose everything."

Caesar didn't respond. Instead, he struck—fast and merciless. His teeth sank into Reynolds' throat, ripping flesh and silencing him mid-breath. The older wolf gasped, eyes wide with agony, hands clawing at the gaping wound. Blood gurgled from his lips as his body spasmed, then collapsed.

Caesar stepped over the lifeless body without a second glance.

Footsteps approached. His ears twitched, muscles coiling as he debated whether to dispatch the driver as well. But luck was with Terry tonight. Without sparing him a glance in the man's direction, Caesar shifted and disappeared into the shadows, retracing his path.

Reynolds wouldn't be the only one to fall. The council needed to be purged. The time had come to tear down the old and make way for the new. He hesitated, considering. He needed something more. A message. Proof of his conviction.

Moving swiftly, he returned to the body. He shifted crouching over the corpse, claws slicing through flesh and tendons with brutal efficiency. He dug, peeled, and severed until only bone remained. With a final, decisive motion, he tore free his trophy. A quick turn. A fleeting shadow. And then he was gone—melding into the night, his grisly prize tucked beneath his arm.

* * *

Evelyn woke to the sound of a baby's cry, sharp and insistent. Her eyes fluttered open to see the nurse from earlier cradling one of the twins, gently motioning for her to lie back down. Exhaustion weighed her limbs like lead, and even the smallest movement sent ripples of pain through her aching body. She let herself sink back into the pillows, but rest would not come.

Despite the crushing fatigue pressing against her chest, a deeper heaviness lingered—something she couldn't shake. Caesar's odd behavior gnawed at her, the shift in his aura unsettling. It felt different.

Darker. And she feared what that meant.

Hera had stayed by her side, chatting, ranting—going on about her brother and her betrothal to Damien. She spoke to Evelyn more in these few hours than she had since stepping foot on the southern shore.

A soft knock at the door pulled Evelyn from her thoughts. She turned to see her husband standing there, smiling.

She inhaled sharply.

His eye. It was healed.

Why hadn't she noticed before?

Caesar stepped closer, catching the confusion in her expression. His smile deepened.

"Checking me out?" he teased, running a hand over his chest, pride swelling in his voice. The thought struck him—he should have done this sooner.

Evelyn sat up slowly, a chill creeping down her spine. She had been too numb, too drained to feel it before, but now the sensation crashed into her like a wave. Magic.

Dark magic.

Her breath hitched.

"What did you do?"

The playful glint in Caesar's eyes dimmed, his mask slipping into place. Doubt. Suspicion.

Anger flared—sudden, sharp, stronger than before.

"Leave us," he commanded, his voice edged in steel. The nurse obeyed without hesitation, tucking the babes to her chest as she slipped out of the room.

Evelyn waited until the door clicked shut before she spoke again, her voice tight.

"What did you do?"

Caesar exhaled sharply and sat beside her, urgency woven into his movements.

"I did what needed to be done." He leaned in, eyes alight with something unreadable. "It was time for a renewal."

He pulled up his shirt, motioning to his chest. "I am renewed," he murmured. "They healed me."

"They? Who are 'they,' Caesar? I will ask again, what did you do?" Evelyn's voice was sharper now, her patience thinning. She wanted an answer. Needed one.

"A healer. Healers." His jaw tightened, searching for words—any words but the truth. The truth would push her away. In time, she would understand.

"These healers—what did they do?" She reached out, her fingertips brushing over his repaired eye, tracing the smooth, unblemished skin.

Caesar smirked.

"Performed a ritual, and bam! Good as new."

Evelyn's hand stilled.

"You're hiding something."

Her pulse quickened as she pulled back, her voice dropping to a whisper. "What was this ritual?"

She swallowed, the weight of dark magic pressing against her senses.

"Caesar, I can feel it. It's all over you. There was more done—what was it? What did you promise them?"

He sighed, catching her wrist before she could fully retreat. He pressed a slow kiss to the delicate skin, but the gesture wasn't soft. It was possessive. Shadows flickered behind his eyes. Visions from the ritual clawed at the edges of his mind, and heat pooled low in his stomach, stirring something darker.

"Nothing for you to worry about." His voice was smooth, assured— too assured. "There was nothing dark about it. My eye is healed. I am reborn. What those witches did—" He exhaled, a quiet chuckle slipping from his lips. "I don't need the Rite of Selene. I am the alpha, and I will take what I want. What we want."

Evelyn held his gaze, but the man staring back at her wasn't the same. His irises flickered, shifting, unstable—like something else lurked just beneath the surface. A shiver ran down her spine.

"Okay."

It was barely a whisper, but it was enough. Enough for him to hear, enough for him to believe she was with him. The details didn't matter. Not now. Maybe not ever.

9

Found

Winston stood horrified, his heart sinking. This was worse than not finding Armand. James had showered and pulled out his funeral suit. Nothing but the best for their alpha. He shook his head, a bitter taste in his mouth. They should have come naked and filthy, like the wretched animals they had become—mere workers, grunt laborers.

He cleared his thoughts and cast a quick glance at Winston. The man looked slightly nervous, and James couldn't fault him; he felt it too as they approached the two guards standing sentinel at the large wooden double doors.

"I would like to request an audience with the alpha." James stood tall, forcing authority into his voice. Winston shuffled slightly beside him. Days had turned into weeks with nothing to show for it, and he wasn't sure what James hoped to gain by asking to see Caesar.

The young brunette to the left cast a lazy, disdainful gaze upon them. Even seated, she seemed to look down her slender, petite nose at them. The male guard said nothing, his expression a mask of poorly veiled disgust. The six-foot blond beside her turned his head, his icy stare landing on Winston.

James wanted to say something but decided against speaking. He didn't want to say anything that might get them both thrown out—or worse.

Winston recognized the man as Norman, a well-known figure in their world of gloom and doom. He heard the stories: heard the rumors of the lives he had taken, the ruthless lengths he would go to fulfill his master's will.

Winston lightly bumped the back of his hand against James' thigh, a warning to tread lightly. James sighed. Moving forward he vowed to find a reliable partner someone that was as passionate as himself.

"Let me see if the Alpha is available to receive visitors."

The young guard didn't wait for acknowledgment; he turned and disappeared behind the heavy door.

"You two should be out in the field." Norman chuckled, running his tongue across his top teeth. "I take it that your presence here means you have news?"

He didn't wait for a response .

"Ah, must be news." He smirked, casting a disdainful eye on the slim manila folder in James' hand. "Because your orders were clear: bring back the bodies of Armand and Amelia. You must have them in that little folder."

The two remained silent, a trickle of fear welling up in Winston's chest. Their orders were clear—crystal. So were the implications of returning empty handed.

"He'll see you both now." The young guard reappeared, watching the pair as they moved forward.

"The alpha will want news." Norman's parting words followed after them.

They fell silent again as the younger guard held the door open. Once they stepped inside, it shut with a dull click, echoing like a closing coffin.

"You two requested an audience." Caesar turned to face them. They recoiled in shock. His eye had been restored, and the aura radiating from him sent shivers down their spines. James instinctively placed his hand behind his back, hiding the folder. The plan slipped from his mind like water through his fingers.

Winston silently hoped James would abandon any social justice protests he had in mind. The change in the man before them made him fear for their lives.

"I am assuming you have news." Caesar drawled coming to stand in front of the large desk.

Winston swallowed audibly. James began stuttering before he finally formed a proper sentence.

"Not yet but we're close. I can feel it." James voice shook as he finished rising on his tip toes.

"You can feel it?" Caesar questioned mockingly. He chuckled his gaze lingering on James. The silenced stretched between them and Winston decided to speak as he felt the energy around them shift.

"Yes. We are close..umm…" he trailed off unsure what to say. He feared too much rambling would provoke their alpha.

Winston began again, "as James said we are close. We've picked up a scent trail. It was faint." He through out quickly. His gaze remained fixed ahead as he watched from his peripheral James's head snap in his direction. They hadn't picked up a scent trail in days but he knew better than to state such.

James re-focused on Caesar and nodded backing up Winston's lie.

"Well, that means you will have results…soon." Caesar leaned forward lingering on the latter part of his statement. "You're dismissed."

Caesar didn't need their response their lives were hanging by a thread, one he considered severing.

They were near the door when Caesar spoke, his voice a low hiss.

"Smart man, James, to table your… grievances." He gestured toward the bent folder in James's hand. "I'm glad you understand your job is to serve, not question. I would hate to put down two of my best scouts."

He paused, a smirk creeping onto his face. "Despite the fact that you haven't produced results."

The two remained rooted in place.

"We will find them." Winston spoke managing to tame the nervousness in his voice.

"See that you do gentlemen."

* * *

Leslie's car groaned in protest, straining to pull them through the mud formed from the first rain of the season. Armand sat in the backseat, gripping Amelia's hand as she leaned forward, navigating their way along the narrow trail off Bear Creek Road.

"Girl, I don't think Sheila's going to make it," Leslie said, reaching forward to pat the dashboard of the old Jeep.

"It shouldn't be too much further. When we get to the lake, we'll have to cross on foot," Amelia said, her gaze drifting out the passenger side window. She had never been here, yet the place felt hauntingly familiar. Something tugged at her, guiding her to this very spot.

"We have to walk in the water? In the mud? Girl…" Leslie lifted her foot slightly, glancing down at her gleaming white canvas Converse, which had only arrived via mail two days ago. "Damn," she whispered, pressing harder on the gas, causing the Jeep to squeal as it bounced over a muddy hole in the road. Leslie was ignored as Amelia's grip on Armand's hand tightened, snapping him out of his trance.

"Amelia?"

"We're close—very close."

She squeezed her eyes shut, her body quivering as if chilled. Amelia wasn't exactly sure where they were headed, but she felt confident enough to guide them. The rest would rely solely on instinct, so she told Leslie to stop. Leslie glanced in the rearview mirror, then stomped on the brakes. The Jeep slid a few feet before coming to a halt.

"Here?" Leslie asked, wide-eyed as she sought confirmation in the mirror, her gaze fixed on her best friend.

"Yes, here. This is it."

Both Leslie and Armand surveyed the barren field, their eyes landing on the creek roughly twenty yards away. Amelia pointed, drawing the attention of her two companions.

"There, we cross there."

They remained silent as they exited the vehicle. Armand moved around to the back to retrieve the duffel bag filled with the items needed for the ritual. He stole a glance upward; darkness was creeping in fast, and stars were beginning to emerge.

"Armand, come on!" Leslie urged, casting a nervous glance over her shoulder at Amelia, who was already ahead of them.

The two jogged to catch up, neither questioning her. Armand instinctively kept his distance from the women establishing a perimeter. A remnant from his early years of training with his father. These woods were foreign, and the sounds echoing around them told of unseen dangers.

Suddenly, Amelia stopped, her eyes vacant and glossy. All three stood at the creek's edge.

"This is the spot," she declared, turning to meet Armand's gaze.

He simply nodded; questions were pointless now. Leslie muttered a quiet "thank God" under her breath, glancing down at her Converse, which were now caked with damp earth. It was nothing a little Mean Green couldn't fix.

Amelia took the bag, and the others watched as she began clearing

FOUND

a spot, moving twigs into strange shapes. Armand knelt to help, but was scolded by Amelia with a sharp snap. The eyes that locked onto his weren't familiar—darker, yet now shimmering with a nearly translucent hue. He slowly stood and stepped back.

"I must be the one to prepare," she said, her voice strained as she pulled items from the bag and arranged them on the ground.

Leslie retreated another step, raising and lowering her shoulders anxiously. She felt a strong urge to pull out her phone and record the moment, but realized she had left it in the Jeep. Glancing around, she understood it wouldn't have been much help anyway; night had fallen, shrouding them in darkness.

As Amelia drew symbols in the dirt, Armand watched intently. They were unfamiliar, yet oddly reminiscent, like something he had glimpsed in a book long ago. Amelia stood, breathing deeply, her lashes brushing against her cheeks. Thunder rumbled overhead, and as if orchestrated, the woods around them fell silent, the wind halting its movement.

"Armand," she whispered, her voice soft and raspy. It wasn't Amelia's, but it was clear his mother was not with them; another presence had inhabited his fiancée. The energy felt different—more powerful. Ancient.

He stepped forward, his movements hesitant as he came to stand beside her. Her speed was like lightning as her hand clasped around his wrist. He gasped at the coldness of her touch, the sensation prickling his smooth skin and he suppressed a shudder. Leslie instinctively moved away, feeling uneasy.

"Here," Amelia instructed, guiding him to stand in front of her before pulling at his clothing until he was completely nude.

"Leave," Amelia hissed, glancing over her shoulder at an unnatural angle. Leslie quickly looked at Armand, who nodded. She returned the gesture and jogged back toward the Jeep.

Once she was out of range, Amelia returned her full attention to

Armand. He held the hazy gaze of his love and watched as she drew a knife from the back pocket of her jeans. He didn't recall her packing it, only surmising she had grabbed it when she went back into the apartment to use the bathroom.

"By the powers of the new moon and the goddess of the wolf, I perform the rite of Selene and endow you with the power of the twelve packs and the great alpha of our kind," Amelia intoned, her words transforming into a song, then a chant.

She raised the blade, bringing the tip to his right shoulder, causing Armand to hiss in pain. He fought to hold his composure as she dragged the blade diagonally across his chest, stopping near his armpit.

The chanting grew louder, and Armand could have sworn he heard howling in the distance. His body felt drained, and he fought against the weakness in his legs, but lost the battle as his knees made contact with the damp soil. His skin burned as if hot coals had been poured across it. He strained to focus on Amelia's chants, which only grew louder as the stillness surrounding them shattered; the woods came alive again. The cicadas' song seemed to synchronize with Amelia's rhythm.

He wasn't sure how long he could hold on to consciousness and momentarily looked up when the woods fell silent once more, and Amelia stopped chanting. Armand gazed into eyes blazing with blood-red fury as she wielded the knife high above her head. He was too weak to move or stop her as she brought the blade down, aiming for the center of his chest. Then, blackness enveloped him as he went limp.

It was dawn when his eyelashes fluttered open, the sun blinding him as he sat up, raising a hand to shield his face. He looked around; he was still in the woods, but there was no sign of Amelia or Leslie.

He stood and wobbled, running his hand along his chest. The wound his brother had left was gone, replaced with smooth skin. The eldest DuBois flexed his muscles, a renewed sense of power surging through his veins, bringing with it fresh rage. He breathed deeply; their scents mingled with that of the creek and the surrounding wildlife. They were still nearby, and he set off in the direction they had come the day before.

As he moved through the tall grass, a buck halted, its large head dropping in acknowledgment before raising its gaze to watch him pass.

He spotted the Jeep ahead and quickened his pace. At the passenger window, he peered inside, watching the two women sleep. He hated to disturb them but lightly knocked on the glass, hoping not to startle them. Leslie raised her head, peering around until her gaze fell on Armand. She shook Amelia, but the young woman only moaned, barely stirring. Abandoning her efforts to wake her friend, Leslie unlocked the door.

"Is she okay?" Armand asked, resting his hand on Amelia.

"I'm not sure; I came back after an hour, and both of you were on the ground. I was able to drag her here, but you," she pointed, "were too damned heavy." She sighed, looking down before meeting her new found friend's gaze.

"How do you feel?"

Armand held Leslie's gaze.

"Better. I want revenge."

Leslie tucked her bottom lip in, nodding. "Okay, well…" She turned in the seat and pressed the engine start button. "Let's get back to Birmingham. Then we can plan." Leslie wasn't sure what she would be able to do, but her willingness was worth something.

Armand shifted Amelia, choosing to ride in the back with her draped across his lap. They rode back to Birmingham in silence. Even when they gained a signal, Leslie quickly snatched at the knob, turning the volume down, a small blue zero appearing in the corner of the screen. Amelia was too tired to keep her eyes open but too restless to sleep, instead silently counted the bumps in the road. Each jolt shook her on a molecular level.

Armand held her close, his hand possessively resting on her hip. Leslie routinely threw glances toward the pair in the backseat. He didn't speak. He couldn't. There was nothing to say.

Instead, he was all feeling. His body tingled, muscles moving beneath his skin, causing tendons to jerk and throb. The sensation didn't bother him; it was fascinating to watch his skin rise and fall as if a ball were rolling along his skeletal frame.

He wasn't sure how Leslie managed to turn an hour trip into thirty-minutes but given that Leslie drove no less than 90 MPH, he wasn't surprised. During the short ride, he had an idea. He just wasn't sure how to go about setting it in motion.

They came in through the back entrance; Amelia cuddled against his chest as he carried her up six flights. Leslie followed behind, wheezing as they cleared the third floor.

Hurriedly, she put the key in the lock, pushing her way over the threshold. He followed, kicking the door shut. He stood concerned as Leslie fished an inhaler from her purse, placing the blue object between her lips. With two quick puffs, she breathed deep, emerging victorious from the battle her lungs had waged against her.

She gave him a quick nod. Satisfied she was well, he laid Amelia on the couch and knelt beside her. Her breathing had improved since the ride up 20/59, and he released a sigh of relief. She had fallen asleep, her eyes too heavy to stay open on their own.

His senses tingled. Someone was near—a threat. He rose. Scouts. Two. He sensed they were young.

"Leslie."

The young woman froze, her gaze violently pulled away from her phone.

"They're here," he whispered, his tone calm. Panic began to show on Leslie's face as she took several shallow breaths in succession.

He held up a large hand. Leslie stopped breathing. The authority in the gesture was enough to quell any outpouring of emotion she had.

* * *

James nodded toward Winston. They had picked up the scent trail; it was strong.

"Through the door."

Winston positioned himself next to it, while James quickly took up the other side.

"Mr. DuBois, I'm here at the request of the alpha. We've been sent to bring you in," James spoke through the door. "It will be better if we bring you and Ms. Anaheim in. Alive."

Winston resisted the urge to shake his head. Had he been with anyone else, they would have gone through the door by now.

Armand moved closer, his left hand outstretched by his side. By this time, Amelia had awoken and sat up, her hands at her temples as her head spun. Leslie fumbled slightly, too scared to move yet too curious to remain completely still.

"What are we waiting for?" Winston asked, ready to charge. James waved him off.

"Something isn't right about this. I can feel it," he said, not bothering to whisper; there was no doubt the man on the other side could hear them. Doubt. At least one of them had it. Armand could use that to his advantage.

"Trust your gut. Why is my brother so anxious to have me dead instead of bringing me before the Elders?" He moved closer. "Think. You're two smart guys. What did I have to gain by killing the man who had already given me the world?"

"Why did you run?" Winston asked.

"To protect my fiancée. To save our lives and come back to save the Coven. My brother will destroy it from the inside out if given the chance. Absolute power is what he is after. If you've met him, I'm sure you've picked up on that."

Silence. Armand didn't hear any rustling nor feel any energetic shifts; they weren't preparing to charge.

"You feel that?" James spoke, his eyes closed. Winston shot him an exasperated look.

"Please, not this again." He stepped closer, speaking directly in James's ear.

"No, but do you feel it? His energy. The power. I don't think we could take him in if we tried." James opened his eyes, his gaze resting on his longtime friend.

"Maybe we should talk to him first." James made the suggestion, but didn't wait for his partner to respond.

"We are coming in," he quickly added, "to talk."

* * *

Leslie sat on the periphery, watching. Listening. Armand had given them a play-by-play of the evening that had transpired weeks prior. It felt like a fantastical tale—almost unbelievable. If she had been told her best friend was a wolf, she would have thought the speaker was on the verge of psychosis and recommended they see her psychology professor for further study.

The two scouts sat bewildered. Winston seemed to be battling his emotions, while James appeared to have accepted what he was being told, his lips pressed into a thin line.

"That's some heavy stuff," James stated as he leaned back in the chair, his legs spreading further.

Leslie's lips down-turned. She didn't want to be the one to point out that the majority of people in the room were naked. The three men seemed so casual about it that she tried to be as well.

"Sounds like some bullshit." Winston stood, placing his empty glass on the counter.

Armand sighed.

The man sitting down, eating a muffin, believed them, but the other was skeptical. It was a good sign; the young man needed all the facts before rendering judgment. Armand was just glad to have gotten them this far without bloodshed.

He was about to interject when a voice cut through the building tension.

"I can show you."

Leslie jumped, and Armand spun on his heel to face Amelia. She was standing a few feet away, and neither of them had noticed her until she spoke.

"Geez," Leslie whispered from the corner. During the conversation, she had moved further away, fearing that more might transpire and not wanting to be caught in the crossfire.

Each scout took one of Amelia's outstretched hands. James quickly let his eyes fall shut, while Winston watched his friend, slightly shaking his head. He just hoped this wouldn't come back to bite them in the ass. He and James would burn with Armand and Amelia if they were found not to have taken down the threat, but something about the man—and about this—made Winston lose some of his skepticism. Although he was not yet a believer. Still, he was willing to listen.

"Winston," Amelia stated, her tone holding so much authority that even Armand took a slight step back. Winston accepted her hand, closing his eyes. He gasped at the flood of images that came to him in flashes. He was in awe, and from the sounds emanating from James, so was he.

When it was over, the two men sat at the small table, engaging in a silent conversation their gazes bouncing back and forth between one another. Winston was the first to speak.

"We will help you two."

James nodded his agreement. "Yeah, what do you need from us?"

Armand was quiet, his mind racing. He couldn't think of anyone he would trust to help. Maybe Charles, but if the man thought Armand had kidnapped his daughter, that would be a no-go. Then someone came to mind.

"My sister. Put me in touch with my sister."

James nodded. "We can do that."

"She's at your parents' place, but we can get to her," Winston said, rising from the table. "In the meantime, all of you need to leave. Russian mercenaries are looking for you two as well." His gaze drifted between Armand and Amelia.

"Russian mercenaries? Damien is here?"

"Yeah, he came for the wedding," James answered, reaching for another muffin. "And from my source…"

"Your nosy cousin," Winston cut in, finally caving and grabbing the last muffin.

James rolled his eyes.

"My source," he leaned forward, emphasizing the point. "Alpha Damien is staying around because he's engaged to your sister. The plan is for her to go back to Russia with him next week."

Armand looked solemn.

If Russian mercenaries were on his trail, that meant they would be here soon. He stole a glance around the room; all eyes were on him. He was their leader. The sensation of spiders dancing on his skin returned. A threat was close. Too close.

"Everyone. Move. NOW!"

10

Dinner

Hera was pulled from her thoughts when the man who had dominated them since his unexpected arrival the previous night stood at her bedroom door. Once again, he wore the same arrogant expression. The confidence radiating from him made her stomach stir, and she bit down on her tongue to provide a distraction.

"Why are you here?" She rose, blocking his path and preventing him from entering her room further.

"Have you forgotten our plans? Dinner. I'm a man who keeps his word, especially to a beautiful woman."

He raked his eyes over the top half of her body, seductive and assured. His gaze alone was enough to melt her resolve, and she let out an exasperated gasp.

Damien chuckled to himself; her defenses were waning, not that the young woman had much of one. He knew her secrets—or at least the ones she hoped would stay buried. He was intrigued, damn near obsessed, which was rare for him when it came to women. It wouldn't be long before she was beneath him or on top of him. His mouth watered at the prospect of what they would do once she surrendered to her darker nature. He would be sure to nurture it.

"I don't want dinner, and I sure as hell don't want you." She rolled her eyes, driving her left foot into the carpet.

His smirk only deepened. "Sure, get dressed... doll."

Hera paused, staring up at him, taken aback by the endearment that rolled off his tongue.

"What did you call me?" she hissed, crossing her arms. "Doll" was a term she reserved for the girls that had been curious but shied away when Hera turned up the heat. Her playthings were dolls not her. She cleared her thoughts, determined not to let him know he could get to her.

"Doll. I called you doll." He stepped closer, eclipsing her petite frame.

"Don't call me that." She whispered, her eyes growing cold.

"Isn't that what you call them? Your dolls? Where do you keep them? In the Pilar building? Do they rotate out, or do you keep them there until they're begging to be let out?" His face was too close, and she stepped back.

"Are you stalking me?"

He stood up straight, letting out a sharp-toothed laugh.

"No, don't flatter yourself. As I've stated before, I know everything about newcomers to my pack—especially those entering the inner circle."

"I'm not joining your pack. The engagement is off."

"Your brother hasn't spoken to me, and given the trade-off, he can't back out of this deal. Not now. Not when I've pulled resources from a business matter to deal with his personal issues." He quirked his eyebrows.

"I don't give a damn about your trade-off. I will not marry you or Alexander. I'm not joining your pack."

He laughed once again. "You are just too adorable."

"Don't patronize me."

"No, I mean it. You're absolutely adorable, and this little show is really

102

too cute. I love the right balance of drama; it keeps life interesting. But I'm afraid, my dear, such theatrics will only be tolerated to a point—and of course, in private. Once we are married, I expect a certain level of restraint and decorum from the matriarch of a coven, especially one as old as mine."

Before she could respond, he stepped back, positioning himself in the doorway.

"Dinner. Don't bother changing; I love to feast on your delectable little body."

She sighed, unable to come up with a response. This man irritated her.

"The staff has already set the table. Hurry, before everything grows cold."

He left, taking off in the direction of the stairs. In a huff, she followed, jogging to catch up with his long strides. The table was magnificent. Two places were set—one at the head and the other on the right side. Outside of a formal occasion, this was proper; as an alpha, his place was naturally deemed to be at the head. He stood behind the chair at the head, pulling it out and staring at her with a smirk on his face.

"I'm not all about tradition; I can have a little fun as well."

Hera rolled her eyes. This wasn't about their laws; with her occupying the head of the table, he positioned himself at the quickest exit available. Strategic. She sat in a huff, pulling the thin robe across her breasts.

In that moment, she noticed how low-cut the pajama top was and made a vain attempt to shield herself from his lustful gaze.

"You don't have to cover yourself for me. Once you and I are married, feel free to walk around naked. My staff are very discreet."

Another eye roll, and Hera motioned for the servers to begin. Best to get on with it and get it over with. She ate quickly, shoving jagged pieces of meat into her mouth. Damien watched, his eyes shifting to a dark grey.

She was a brat—spoiled, entitled—but he expected nothing less from a third-born, especially a daughter. An only daughter. That wasn't what intrigued him. He could have his pick of the litter, so to speak. There were several first-borns he could take to further strengthen his reach and power.

Naturally, with anyone who came into his pack, he vetted them. It was his way of tilling his garden, removing the weeds before they could take root, and he had done so with Hera. On the surface, she was boring—a perfect match for his equally uninteresting cousin. But dig deeper, and that's where he found the skeletons: the girl quitting school and returning home all of sudden.

Then there were the families that disappeared entirely. That wasn't alarming, given who her father had been; he was protecting his own. But a deeper dive revealed rumors surrounding the young woman's sexual proclivities. They bordered on perversion, some even pushing beyond that boundary.

A young classmate of his intended had been forthcoming as she rubbed the rope burns around her wrist and the one around her neck as she recalled their encounter. It was innocent enough initially the two girls engaging in a little freshman experimentation before Hera suggested more. Sarah's pain was Hera pleasure. The youngest DuBois had gotten off on watching the young woman struggle nearly unconscious as Sarah dangled from the ropes.

His advisor had been present as the American told all she knew of Hera. His uncle later spoke against bringing a woman such as Hera into their pack. But he had been intrigued possibly obsessed; Hera's appetites were similar to his own, and given enough time, his fiancée would see that as well. She would come to understand that he was a safe space. An outlet.

Silence enveloped them, pressing against her bosom, and Damien was determined to let her wallow in it. The way her leg bounced and her eyes touched everything but him was telling. She was agitated. It was the energy—primal, sexual—and he fought the urge to clear the table and toss her on it. But if she wanted to play this game, then he would oblige.

"Do they not feed you?"

"What?"

"Your brother—is he telling the staff not to feed you? You're eating like a starved child."

She roughly picked up a roll and shoved it into her mouth.

He chuckled, grabbing one and mimicking her actions. With a deep eye roll, she swallowed the chewed food, letting her fork fall with a thump against the table.

"Why are you doing this?" She crossed her arms, causing her breasts to lift. His eyes darted down toward them before rising to meet hers.

A change. Ah, there she is—the woman he wanted was slowly making an appearance. Seductress was the only thing he could classify her as, right before his eyes.

"I thought since we are engaged, it would be fitting for me to court my wife-to-be. Dinner is a great place to start unless," he closed his eyes and took a deep breath, opening them slowly. They were now a deep blue. "You have other ideas?"

He was insufferable, which set her skin ablaze. This dinner was difficult in more ways than she could count. Her body was once again unruly, and she wanted to punish herself. But those thoughts led to something else—a slickness between her thighs. She could smell her arousal and was sure he could as well. It was subtle, but he shifted, seeming to slide to the edge of his chair and closer to her.

She wanted to leave the room, and if necessary, she would leave the building. Anything to escape him. He brought out the side of her she fought to keep hidden. Hera had sought to explore her urges, to act in accordance with her nature, and in the process, several people had gotten hurt. Her dolls were always eager and willing to play. It was only after they saw how dark the fantasies were and how far she wanted to go that they—her dolls—wanted to stop.

She looked away first. Her pride urged her not to be the one to break, but she had to. In that moment, a brush of fingers would have sent her clawing at his suit and gnawing on his full lips.

Damien was too aroused to appreciate this small victory. He stood abruptly, all he had wanted to discuss, to ask, to reveal forgotten. There would be other times for fact-finding. Her guard was down, but so was his. In such a position, it was better not to proceed.

"Good night."

He left, exiting nearly like a shadow. Hera only watched, letting out a breath of frustration—or was it anger? She wasn't sure which.

11

Evidence

"Do you have evidence?" The elder councilman moved closer. Charles stopped talking, grunting a reply.

"Some."

"What in the hell does that mean?"

"I have enough for a formal inquiry."

Pierce hissed, holding onto Charles' lapel. Charles regarded him, unwilling to reveal all he had uncovered. He couldn't without exposing his own actions. Hera was his only play.

Charles had pieced together enough information, including tracking down Armand's elusive former assistant, Tina. She had practically vanished, but through a few distant relatives, he managed to locate her and uncover what she knew.

During their time together, a chilling thought slithered into his mind—what if he rid their world of her? The woman knew too much.

He quickly banished the thought. Tina had been discret; faded into obscurity with no fanfare. She posed no threat, and Charles was no longer a man who killed in the name of the coven or his alpha.

Those days were buried in the past. Once he dealt with Caesar and cleared Armand's name, he and his family would leave. The engagement of his daughter and Armand was as good as over in his mind. The very idea of remaining with the coven drained him. Aiding in its genesis had devoured the doctor's soul. He refused to let the propagation of it take his daughter's as well.

The night before, Charles meticulously arranged the contents inside a large envelope. He had wrestled with the decision on whom to address it to. Who could he trust to make a difference, to steer things in the right direction?

A council member was out of the question; they would surely betray him for a shot at Caesar's favor. And Reynolds? The elder had fallen silent, vanished, his phone going straight to voicemail. That didn't bode well. Reynolds always answered on the first ring, second if he was busy, and third if he was asleep.

Then an unexpected name surfaced in his mind—Hera. A wild card, certainly, but unlike her brothers, she had a knack for asking the right questions and demanding answers. Perhaps that was why Caesar wanted her off the continent.

Her engagement hadn't reached the others on the council, but Charles had insight—and more importantly, he had ears and eyes in Damien's camp.

His attention returned to Pierce as the tall rail thin man released him, huffing.

"You better take your seat. They'll be arriving shortly. I suggest you don't mention this to anyone." He held his finger to Charles' nose, nearly touching the tip.

Charles was about to speak, but the words died on his lips as the men tumbled in like unsorted laundry. Quiet anger and veiled annoyance pulsed through each man, summoned from their beds in the wee hours of the morning.

Caesar entered and stood at the head of the table, his eyes glowing dimly as the men took their usual places at his sides. Charles settled into the chair directly opposite him. The doctor noted the chair usually occupied by Reynolds was empty. Silence and tension hung heavy around them; it was clear forces beyond this realm were at play. Many had borne witness to the same in Samuel.

* * *

Hera stared at the package, suspicion swirling in her mind. She initially thought about tossing it in the trash, convinced it was from Damien, but curiosity got the better of her. With a swift tear, she ripped it open, revealing letters, papers, and death certificates. The bizarre contents made her scrunch her face, her lips forming a tight ball of tinted flesh.
Charles.
The name flickered at the edge of her consciousness. Although the package offered no indication of the sender she could easily conclude it was him. She thought of his impromptu visit. The move was very uncharacteristic of the man raising her suspicions. Yet somehow, the more she thought of him and her family inconsequential things; memories, words that had little to no connection seemed to align.
She was confused unwilling to come to the conclusion that there was a possibility that Caesar lied, and despite his talks of righteousness he was just like the others she heard about. The alphas that took their power by force and spilled innocent blood in the quest of it. Pieces of a puzzle were starting to assembly revealing a disturbing portrait of her second brother. If Armand was indeed innocent and Caesar the cause of all of the upheaval he would need to be stopped.
She eyed her bag. Inside where the pills that allowed her to forget – to dream. Before she fell down the rabbit hole, another man invaded her thoughts.

Damien.

He was her betrothed, after all; he had an obligation to her. She dialed the number on the card. He answered on the second ring.

"Hello?"

Hera hesitated, doubt creeping in about her decision to seek his help. The silence stretched, and she wished for him to hang up.

"You playing phone tag is a little dated, don't you think?"

Hera smirked, though her expression quickly shifted.

"I…need you."

"Well, that's surprising to hear. I must admit, I'm quite pleased by your admission. Tell me more."

She detected the teasing lilt in his voice.

"Not in that way. I need your help."

He didn't brother pressing for more. It didn't matter, "I'm on my way."

"No! It's better if I come to you. I… where are you?"

"No need. I'll come and pick you up. I don't want you out alone with everything that's happening."

The line went dead before Hera could voice any further protest. Thirty minutes later, she found herself in the passenger seat, heading away from the city. Damien sped down Hwy 280, wrestling with the urge to place his hand on Hera's bare thigh. He was curious about what she needed his help with, though it hardly mattered. She could have asked him to wrangle the Moon from its orbit, and he would have found a way.

They passed through a gate, and Damien slowed as he navigated the winding driveway to a sprawling home. After parking, he shut off the engine and stepped out of the vehicle. Hera sat motionless, her mind racing with doubt. Had she made a mistake coming to him? Another alpha. Yet, she had nowhere else to turn. She didn't want to believe Charles or his claims, but he seemed sincere, and the evidence he had presented—she could only assume the envelope was from him—was undeniably compelling.

Long, strong fingers hovered just inside the open door. She glanced at them before shifting her gaze to Damien. The hunger from dinner lingered, and she knew this was a bad idea. She took the offered hand, neither of them speaking until they made in the house and to an office.

"Now that we are here, what can I do for you at this late hour?"

He lowered his gaze, the darkness amplifying the richness of his eyes. Hera didn't bother countering his suggestive tone; instead, she shoved the thick envelope forward.

Confusion flashed across Damien's face as he rolled his eyes. He had dismissed two blondes earlier, expecting the young woman to seek him out after dinner. Damien hissed softly—this wasn't what he had in mind. He accepted the envelope after she impatiently shoved it toward him, hands on her hips.

As he skimmed through the contents, Hera's expression fell; the fire that burned within her upon entering his home had long been extinguished. He watched her from hooded eyes, feeling a twinge of sadness at seeing her so deflated.

His confused gaze settled on her as he held the envelope out from his body.

"What is this?"

She took a steadying breath and gave him an overview of everything he held in his hand. Hera had scanned the information, but it felt incomplete—something was missing. Unsure of which questions to ask, she trusted Damien and shared everything she knew, carefully avoiding any mention of Charles. For now, she would keep that confidence.

Damien listened intently as she spoke of her coven and its secrets. Her concerns confirmed his suspicions about Caesar. He had heard rumors about the DuBois family. Damien was well acquainted with the tales of her father and his rise to power.

Her voice shook and she wobbled reaching out for comfort. He dropped the packet and gently engulfed her in his arms. The façade of strength was gone as she began to tremble, succumbing to tears.

She looked up at him with large watery orbs. Damien swore he would have fallen into them if they hadn't already sunk to the floor. She placed a delicate hand on his chest. His racing heart matched the rhythm of her own. As his lips touched hers, it felt right. The idea of being bound to him didn't sound as outrageous as it had before.

Damien broke the kiss and rose, pulling her up with him. In one quick motion, she was in his arms and, with long strides, he headed out of the office and toward the stairs.

He placed her on the bed and stood looking down at her.

"No games. I must know, do you want this? I have never taken a woman that was unwilling, and I don't plan to start now. So I must know, is this what you want?"

Hera nodded, pulling at her shirt. He reached down, stopping her.

"Your words. I need to hear you say it."

He knelt to be leveled with her. She searched his eyes. This was the first time she sensed vulnerability. Her consent was important to him.

"Yes, I want you," Hera said as she gently touched his left cheek. She paused, which caused him to withdraw. He considered that this might have been a bad idea. He started to get up but was stopped by her firm grip on his forearm.

"Do you want me? Do you really want me? I'm not a good person." Hera whispered her gaze betraying insecurity.

Damien observed she appeared apprehensive. If she thought he would be put off by this admission, she was mistaken. He did not consider himself a good person, either.

"Yes, since I first saw the pictures of you. I was jealous you had chosen my cousin." He swallowed hard uncomfortable with the bit of vulnerability he had displayed.

She gave him a faint smile.

"I'm not a good person either, Hera. Never have been."

His words put her at ease, and she guided his lips to hers. With that one kiss, he was hooked, and from there he took the lead.

"Mark me." Her voice was so low Damien leaned in closer afraid he'd misheard.

"Mark me." She repeated louder barely above a whisper.

There was no mistaking her words his mind flashed to Giselle and the way her lips had moved when she had spoken the same command. But the woman was lost to him; gone to be with the ancestors.

Heat stirred low in his belly and his breathing became labored. His dick became even more strained causing him pain. It was begging to be released, to be inside her.

"Damien, mark me." She spoke harsher her irises growing dark, they had become two small abysses and Damien longed to lose himself in them.

He drew his lips back his fangs growing in length.

"No."

He was confused; this was the way. This was their way. The way of his father and hers. She pushed him back and rose moving toward the desk in the room. Hera picked up the letter opener and brought it to Damien placing it in his hand.

"Mark me." She had spoken the command a third time finally his brain turned back on and he took control. She was surrendering to him.

She wanted dominance. Pain. He would be more than happy to oblige. He grabbed her by the upper arm forcibly turning her around before he shoved her onto the bed. Hera laid face down her body shaking in anticipation of what was to come a flood of moisture coated her upper thighs as he brought the blade to the fleshy part of her left butt cheek.

His breathing became labored, and he quickly sought out some form of self-control. When he was finished he placed a kiss on the exposed flesh blood coating his lips. His tongue darted out tasting the liquid.

Hera hissed when his warm tongue made contact with the raw wound. The sensation was short lived as Damien flipped her onto her back settling between her legs. She brought her hands to his face running them over his upper body trying her best to touch everything all at once. She wanted to remember the contours of his hard firm body, the marks on his back.

Damien supported himself above her and didn't bother stopping her. Usually this much contact was a no. Not since Giselle had he allowed a woman to touch him beyond what was necessary for his release and during those moments the women were usually bound.

In a swift gentle motion he was inside of her. He gripped the sheets beside them composing himself holding back his release.

Hera arched into him her eyes closing as he began to move the young woman chided herself that she was unable to keep her eyes open. Her grip tightened on his shoulders as he went harder. Deeper.

"I need more." She spoke breathless.

"What do you need?" He stated through gritted teeth. He was nearing the peak and fought desperately not to fall off.

Hera didn't speak and kept her eyes shut tight as she reached for his hands and brought them to her neck. Damien got the meaning and placed light pressure as he began to move again. His strokes slower and more deliberate as he kept his gaze fixed to the changing expressions fluttering across her face.

The alpha applied more pressure. He continued for several minutes alternating between restricting air and cutting it off completely.

He noticed with the latter the woman beneath him clenched around his manhood tighter and Damien enjoyed the game.

Before long he pounded into her with one hard final stroke before grunting and collapsing on top of her still inside as her walls pulsated around him. Milking him. Hera's body shook and she brought her hands up to Damien's back digging her nails into his flesh. He braced himself and hissed proud to add the scars to the others prominently displayed on his back. She had drawn blood, Damien could tell as the scent lingered between them and he could feel the air hitting the small wounds.

"You belong to me now Hera." He whispered grabbing a hand full of hair pulling her head back. Her gaze was on him as she wore a small smirk.

"And you to me."

* * *

She had intended to leave, and Damien even had the driver bring around the car. She had a few more desires sated before he told her enough and that more, better, was to come. She instinctively rubbed her thighs together; his head had been between them only moments before on the hood of the car.

The driver did his best to look everywhere but the alpha and his bride to be. Attempting to go home was futile and quickly forgotten as Damien carried her into the house and back upstairs both of them shedding what little remained of their clothes. Rounds two and three was even more taxing and Hera's body ached and the bruising around her wrists and ankles were becoming more prominent.

The night with Damien was remarkable, but reality always brought with it the undesirable, and the package along with its secrets came back to her consciousness.

Her brother was a traitor, and her father murdered—a truth she would have to confront on her own. With their wedding looming and the memory of giving Damien her virginity just hours ago, she felt a storm of conflicting emotions.

Damien sensed her uneasiness and pulled her closer. He was many things, but as an alpha, he tolerated little. He had zero patience for traitors, especially when it came to family and the inner circle. Blood was everything; any hint of disloyalty had to be eradicated without hesitation.

The weight of his thoughts pressed down on him. Caesar needed to be extinguished. Damien knew he couldn't take any part in the act without igniting a war and losing the woman in his arms. He needed to find Armand—alive.

12

Unpleasant Memories

Maximillian *sighed, hoping the more distance he created between himself and his second son, the less he would have to say—and the less he would have to hurt him. His coldness was meant to protect the boy, but Caesar was persistent, his footsteps echoing Maximillian's own.*

"Father, please," he begged, striving to keep his voice low as they moved through the building's lobby.

Maximillian quickened his pace, and Caesar couldn't help but admire his father's agility as he sidestepped a janitor, despite knowing how sick he was.

A few curious eyes lingered on him, their sympathetic gazes stinging.

He hated it.

* * *

It was a reflex—another nightmare. Like the previous nights, Evelyn reached toward his side, expecting the warmth of his pale flesh to extinguish her fears and doubts. But he wasn't there. The bed felt unnaturally cold, and she pulled the covers up to her chin in vain.

Evelyn attempted to go back to sleep, but she knew it was futile. Slowly, she rose and grabbed her gown from the foot of the bed, quickly covering her naked form. She stood still, straining to hear anything, but cursed when she was met with silence.

"Damn soundproofing." Her gaze fell on the baby monitor on the nightstand—it was off, and a wave of worry began to choke her.

She exited the master bedroom, her eyes drifting toward the nursery. The door was ajar, and she heard faint sobs. She rushed forward but slowed as she neared. It was him—her husband.

She stared at the threshold, watching and waiting, unsure of what for, but anticipation held her captive.

He sensed her presence before she even left the bedroom; it was eerie. His gift was becoming a curse, further locking him in his own mind. He wanted to confide in her, to trust her as he had before, but he couldn't. He shouldn't. How would she react to what he had done? Could he bear her wrath? Her pain?

"Do you love them, Evelyn?" He asked, the question hung heavy in the air filling the space between them. It carried so much history that Evelyn wasn't sure how to respond. She watched as he cuddled the boys closer against his chest almost as if he was afraid she would snatch them from him and vanish.

"Equally, I mean?"

It was the first time he had looked at her since she entered the nursery. His expression carried such a sadness that she had to shift her gaze away from his.

"Of course. I love them both; they are equal in my eyes. All of that first born and second born nonsense doesn't matter. At least it doesn't with us."

She approached and knelt, coming to eye level with her husband.

Their boys were asleep, and for Caesar, the sight was too close, too reminiscent of his own childhood. Secretly, he had hoped for daughters, wanting to avoid the cruel fate of having a son tied to their family's dark past. With girls, there was inherent importance; neither would be born purely to serve the elder.

"I did something," he whispered, rocking the boys against his chest. Evelyn's heart raced; she feared he would suffocate them both if she didn't intervene.

Gently, she placed her hands on his arms, staring into his eyes, which were red and glassy. She couldn't get over the transformation. His left eye, once clouded, now gleamed with clarity, and his skin glowed, taut and alive. His body had a firmness she wasn't accustomed to; she had never seen anything like it—at least not here, not in America.

"What did you do, my love?" She held her breath, hoping that by depriving herself of oxygen she might wake up from this nightmare.

"I…" He faltered, looking down at their sleeping boys, unsure how to confess that he had promised one of them away to the Two Sisters of all creatures. He had reached a new low, and he couldn't pinpoint when he had fallen so far.

"Tell me, my love," she said in a gentle voice, attempting to hide her growing fear. A chill crawled up her spine despite the layer of perspiration blanketing her skin. The thin silk gown was damp with sweat, sticking uncomfortably to her body.

"You wouldn't love me anymore if I did."

"That's not true. I would. I would still love you," a small lie but one that needed to be told. She steeled herself for the worst.

He didn't wait long before he let the words tumble out, "I promised the Sisters one of them; the stronger of the two," he averted his gaze he would drive the blade in all at once quickly bringing the heartbreak.

Evelyn remained silent unwilling to acknowledge his darker nature, the same side of him that had tethered them together. In the beginning, it is what ignited her attraction for him now it terrified her. She was sleeping with a monster.

Evelyn stood, heat radiating from her body. The sudden shift in her energy triggered something primal within him, and he was on his feet in an instant. The urge to kill, to destroy, surged within him, and he bit down on his tongue, tasting blood. Shame washed over him—ashamed of the thoughts threatening to spill into actions that could harm, that could kill. He stood there, staring at her, drinking in Evelyn's rage; her pain was intoxicating, and he reached for the crib for support.

Evelyn tightened her grip on their boys.

"Why did you do that?" Her voice barely above a whisper.

"I did what I had to do. The Two Sisters—they had a price."

"The Two Sisters?" Confusion flickered across Evelyn's face; she had never heard of such beings. Yet she held back her questions, allowing him the space to reveal more.

"They're witches, Evelyn. Witches. Black magic. I sought them out for help, hoping they could give me what I needed to shift the odds in our favor, but…" He stepped closer, wrapping his arms around her rigid body.

"I did this for us, Ev, and for them." He murmured, glancing down at the babes cradled in her arms.

With a slow, deliberate motion, she freed herself from his grasp.

"You did this for yourself. How could you?" She scanned the room, the anger melting away, leaving only pain. Fear.

"Ev, have a little faith in me. I'm not actually going to give him away. I just needed them to believe that. That's all."

"That's even worse. You've never dealt with their kind before. There are severe consequences for not honoring your word."

"I'll simply kill them. That was the plan all along." He questioned his own conviction, uncertainty gnawing at him. He was well aware of the rumors swirling among their kind regarding those who failed to keep their promises to the Sisters; they always got their due, one way or another.

Her doubtful gaze never left him as she pulled the boys closer and retreated from the room. Whatever plans her brother had to aid her needed to be expedited; she just didn't know how she could escape. With this newfound power, Caesar could track her. She had no doubt that he would hunt them to the ends of the earth.

She feared that even her brother—despite his power and knowledge of the occult—might not stand a chance.

He lingered in the nursery, staring at the empty crib. Slowly, he made his way back to the bedroom, disappointed not to find his family there.

Disappointment was familiar, it was home and wondered why he ever felt things would be different. Their empty bed stood as a symbol of the state of his life. Empty. Disheveled. The scene triggered a memory; one he had fought hard to suppress over the years but always won out playing on a loop until a bottle of Jack Daniels made it stop.

* * *

"Father?"

Maximillian glanced up from the papers in his hand, his expression shifting from sadness to a faint scowl as he set the thin sheets face down on his desk.

"Yes?"

Annoyance tinged his tone—not quite anger, but close enough.

"I heard about Armand's...presentation."

A long sigh escaped the older man, his shoulders slumping inward.

"He told you."

"Yes, Armand has been quite forthcoming about his desire not to become Alpha. So..." He trailed off, bracing himself for the impending storm that was his father's response.

121

"As I've told your brother and your mother, it doesn't matter whether he wants to be alpha or not. He is the eldest, the firstborn son. It is his duty. You, as the second-born, are to serve as beta to your brother. Serve and perform the unsavory tasks that come with absolute authority."

"That's the problem. I was born to be more than a lackey to someone who doesn't even want the role. You can choose. As alpha, you have that right. I've read our laws and consulted with key council members no one would oppose you appointing someone to take your place."

He took a deep breath to steady himself, using the pregnant pause to steal a quick glance at his father. Tired. Resigned. Those were the words that defined the man before him. He pressed on before the tide shifted.

"It would break with tradition, but there is precedent. No one would question your authority if you were to choose...me." He smiled—not his usual toothy grin, but one tinged with uncertainty that prompted Maximillian to raise an overgrown eyebrow.

Caesar lowered his gaze and watched the shift in his father's demeanor. He planted his feet, bracing for the hurricane he knew was about to make landfall. He was just surprised he hadn't invoked his father's ire sooner.

"Hmm. I was hoping..." Maximillian's voice trailed off, frustration knitting his brows. "I promised your mother I would spare your feelings, that I wouldn't have to endure this same conversation I witnessed my father have with my younger brother when he thought he could lead."

"You, my son Caesar, are not ready, nor are you fit. If you were, then with Armand's renunciation of his birthright, I would be lucky to have another male child waiting in the wings. But that's not the case. You are egotistical, and dare I say, at times, maniacal. Impatient and arrogant—leadership is not your strong suit. As a second-in-command, you are perfect. You already thrive in the shadows my boy, so managing the Coven's dirty work will be an easy task. Once your brother is alpha you must make sure he keeps a safe distance from any misdeeds that an alpha can not afford to be near. Accept it: you are a beta. You should be thankful there are worse fates for a second *born male."*

Maximillian stood, watching tears well up in his son's eyes. Caesar stared past him, lost in a haze of disappointment. He'd have to explain this to Hemesh. He could only hope his son would stop asking, cease the useless quest to be more, to do more than what was required and expected.

"I..." Caesar's voice cracked, and he paused, swallowing hard. "I have prepared for this. For the role. How can you say these things to me? I am more than ready. I am capable, and above all, I want this more than he does— more than he ever did!" He shouted, his voice trembling with desperation, hoping to shake reason into the old man.

"Your preparation has been in vain." Maximillian picked up the papers from earlier, a new expression washing over him—worry.

Caesar remained rooted in place, determined to hold his ground until his father truly saw him and the man he had become.

Maximillian waited, hoping his silence would be enough for dismissal. But he had to voice what he wished he wouldn't.

"Making you alpha," he glanced at his son, the dampness on Caesar's cheeks only aggravating him further, "would be like making Hera alpha. I'd have better luck with her, despite all her imprudence."

The dismissal was harsh. His words sliced through the air, leaving Caesar wounded, a hiss escaping his lips as the pain cut deep.

The second-born left just as he had come, his head hung low as he bypassed his mother, who waited at the bottom of the stairs. He refused to beg. If his father didn't see his value then he would make him. Caesar would bring this fragile kingdom crashing down around them all.

* * *

The memory stopped there but the pain only rose in intensity. He wouldn't chase her like he had done with his father in the lobby all those years ago. Caesar fell into the tumbled sheets the memories and his fears forgotten.

13

New Allies

The scouts kept their word and found his sister. As they waited for an audience with the coven's princess, the two men took in the lush surroundings, their eyes sweeping over the vibrant foliage.

Angela waited with them; assessing the odd visitors, her gaze betraying a thinly veiled odium. The sharp angles of her chiseled face revealed nothing else as she turned on her heel, moving swiftly down a long hallway and toward the stairs.

"You have visitors." The young housekeeper knocked lightly, not waiting for a response before entering. Hera glanced up from where she was studying the marks around her wrists.

Her first night with Damien had turned into another session. This was different; unlike before she a willing participant who knew what to do. He understood her needs and had given her the dominance she craved.

"Yes," she hissed, irritation bubbling to the surface at being pulled from her daydreams.

"Visitors, ma'am. Scouts." The woman nodded, her eyelids nearly fluttering closed.

"Send them in."

"I can wait until you dress. Ma'am, it's improper for them to come in here."

"Send them in!" Hera shouted, rising onto her knees. The sudden movement tipped over the plate, spilling an untouched breakfast across the floor.

"Yes." The housekeeper exited quickly to fulfill her mistress's command, keeping her gaze downward as she quickly made her way downstairs. Angela passed her mother who had stopped dusting to shake her head at her daughter.

"I told you," the older woman remarked as Angela hurried by, avoiding her scolding gaze.

Angela entered the room to find the two scouts by the window. The smaller of the two seemed captivated by the view, while the other appeared embarrassed, his mouth set in a tight line.

"She will see both of you now."

Hera quickly pulled on a sweatshirt, ignoring her bare legs, still clad in the shorts she had slept in when Damien brought her home.

"James and Winston, ma'am," Angela announced, glancing between the two men. She lingered at the threshold, aware it was not proper for a young woman—especially the alpha's sister—to be in the presence of men, let alone two, without another party present.

Hera sighed; she loathed protocol and couldn't understand why this young woman was so bound by it.

"Angela, you can leave."

"Yes, ma'am." The housekeeper gave a small curtsy, eliciting a rare smile from Hera. She would be perfect. They waited until the door clicked shut behind Angela, ensuring she was out of earshot.

Hera sighed, already annoyed and chiding herself for taking visitors. The thought of her young maid would have to wait; she intended to explore a certain path further when she was once again alone.

"Speak."

James cleared his throat, nerves prickling at the back of his mind. Though Hera was small, he sensed dark intentions, and he knew it was best to finish quickly and leave.

"Your brother sent us."

She clicked her tongue, leaping from the bed.

"Enough. Out. Tell my brother he can go to hell."

"Wait. Wait." Winston held out his hands. "Hear us out. Your brother Armand sent us."

She wanted to dismiss this as a joke, some kind of test. Caesar was testing her, as if she were a common minion rather than one of the DuBois bloodline. She would make him pay for so blatantly challenging her loyalty.

"Tell Caesar that there's no need to test my loyalty. Also, tell him I'm not amused. I'm not staying here. I'll be leaving by Friday to return to school."

"You have every right not to believe us. We are strangers. Scouts. But I assure you, Armand sent us. He is alive, and he didn't do what they're claiming he did." James hoped his sincerity came through in his voice.

"I don't believe you." She whispered, casting a suspicious glance over his frame. "I could have you killed for spreading lies. Treason. Yes, treason is what Caesar would call it."

James did most of the talking while Winston stood beside the door, taking in the woman. She was petite and pretty, but something lurked beneath the surface—something dangerous, licentious. Winston had been around long enough to recognize her kind. The Coven's code of conduct was reserved for the inferiors; those in power didn't have to abide by such inconveniences.

* * *

"Ah, the infamous Armand. Wow, you're not the same since the last time I saw you—what was it, over ten years ago? Hmm, how you got past my guards is a mystery. I'll have to dispense with them." He held up his hand. "But I sense forces beyond this realm are at play here." He dropped his hand to his side.

"You could say that."

"You've got some real balls showing up here, especially since you're a wanted man. I could drop you now, no questions asked. You sent back the heads of two of my best and most feared mercenaries. Now, Armand, what do I tell the families of these men?"

"What you tell their families is of no concern to me. Besides, they died in the line of service. The families can take comfort in that."

Damien chuckled.

"Then what is your concern? I'll have you know I have no qualms with you, Armand. As far as this matter goes, you did nothing wrong. So what? You got rid of the old man ahead of schedule." He raised and lowered his shoulders, leaning into the desk.

He carefully picked up the glass resting on its edge.

"But then again, haven't we all moved obstacles out of our way to speed things along. Your case is nothing special."

Damien took a sip and waited for Armand to speak.

"I didn't do it. I didn't kill my father or mother."

"Don't care if you did or didn't. But let's be clear, Armand." Damien pushed himself off the desk, standing up straight, the glass at his side.

"You came here. To me. Now, I'll be straight with you: the only reason I took this little meeting is because of your sister. She is my intended, so I granted this small request. What is it that you want, Armand?"

The words hung heavy in the air. Armand didn't want to say it, but Damien could deliver him Caesar, and the Russian knew it.

"I'll speak plainly. I need your help, but you knew that already."

Damien gave a sly grin before taking another sip.

"I did."

"What will it cost me?"

Damien playfully tapped his chin with a long index finger.

"Hmm, let me think, let me think. I don't know."

Armand huffed, rolling his eyes.

"You don't know? I don't believe you."

"No, you shouldn't. But since you need my help gaining access to your brother, you'll have to settle for not knowing."

He shook his head.

"I can't do that. Give you, of all people, a blank check? Nah."

"You don't have a choice." Mirth danced in Damien's deep baritone voice.

"Fine. But don't make me regret it." Armand sighed weighing his limited options.

"Trust me, you won't. Besides, I wouldn't go against a man who has tapped into ancient magic." He pointed a long finger at Armand. "Don't deny it. It vibrates creating ripples, a disturbance on a still lake."

"Real poetic."

Damien chuckled, recognizing the jest in Armand's tone.

"Oh yeah, I'm a real Pushkin." His expression fell the lighthearted moment gone as quickly as it came.

"Well, have a seat. Any ideas, Armand, on how we go about this hostile takeover?"

14

Fading

Damien walked in, but stopped halfway to Caesar's out-stretched arms.

"Brother! How's everything?" He took in Damien's shocked expression and closed the gap. The Russian remembered himself, schooling his features as he embraced the new alpha.

"I'm doing well. I would like to take your sister with me when I return home."

"Ah, brother, sit first." Caesar gestured to the leather sofa, snapping his fingers at a young butler in the corner.

"Brandy," he said, then focused back on Damien. "Then business."

Damien complied, sinking into the soft, firm leather. Moments later, the young man offered a tray holding two half-full glasses. Caesar took them both, handing one to Damien. He sat next to him, his mint-green eyes bright and glossy. Damien looked away. He refused to get lost in the man's dark gaze. The black magic radiated leaving its fingerprints on everything in its path.

Caesar broke the silence.

"I have been healed. My eye restored. Would you like to touch it?" He didn't wait for a response before grabbing Damien's free hand and placing it over his restored eye.

"Feel," Caesar pressed Damien's hand firmly against his skin, slightly depressing the eyeball.

"It's real. Not glass. They healed me. Maybe I can take you." He pointed to the scar on Damien's left cheek. It was small, but stood out against the smoothness of the rest of his tanned skin.

Damien's fingertips burned, and he slowly pulled back his hand. Caesar laughed.

"I know. That's something I'm still getting used to. Evelyn kicked me out of bed last night. Said I was too hot," he exaggerated, bucking his eyes. "Too hot—like that's even a thing."

He stood, spreading his arms and taking a few small steps back.

"What do you think? Huh?" He spun around, allowing his future brother-in-law to take in the view. The new man.

"New and improved. You look well, Brother."

Caesar bowed. "Well, thank you." He sat heavily on the sofa, leaning into the backrest.

"What do I owe the pleasure of your visit? I thought you and my sister would be leaving this weekend. Why the delay?" The playfulness of the moment was gone. It was replaced by a heaviness that Damien couldn't place.

"I was thinking of a going-away party, first. You, the council, and several key influential members of your coven to celebrate."

"The betrothal of a third-born is hardly news worth celebrating. What's the real reason, Damien? Or do you take me for a fool?" Caesar rose to his feet, his gaze hard as he looked down at the Russian.

"Maybe to you, a third-born may not mean much, but in my culture, any upcoming wedding is something to celebrate. Hera is your father's only daughter... your only sister. Surely you want to honor this big moment for her. She's a third-born marrying an alpha—how often does that happen in our world, hmm?" Damien stood, placing an arm around Caesar.

"Besides, when do we ever need a real reason to party?" He playfully bumped Caesar on the chest with a closed fist.

"Armand."

Damien's expression remained cool, though he felt as if he had been made.

"Do you have news of Armand? Are your mercenaries closing in?"

Damien chuckled to himself, realizing this would be the perfect lure to ensure Caesar's attendance.

"Maybe this party isn't all about my betrothal," he whispered in Caesar's ear. "Perhaps I didn't want to spoil the surprise."

"You have Armand?"

Damien stepped out of their half-embrace, looking down demurely at his untouched brandy.

"Pieces."

Caesar's expression shifted to one of glee, his eyes lighting up with delight. Damien locked his knees, feeling a shiver of unease as he focused on keeping his expression neutral.

"Why didn't you say so, Brother?"

"You know me well enough, Caesar. I'm a master of the art of the tease." He bowed, mimicking his host's earlier gesture.

Standing upright, he added, "I assume Hera and I can count on you to attend?"

"Of course. I'll make sure everyone is there."

"Good." Damien raised his glass. "To Alpha Caesar."

Caesar mirrored the gesture, raising his own glass. "To me."

* * *

Evelyn held the shells, giving them a light shake before tossing them onto the mat. This was the fourth time she had done this, and each toss revealed nothing good. They only confirmed what she already knew evil lurked around her.

Footsteps echoed in the hallway. She quickly grabbed the shells and slipped them into a small, unmarked pouch.

"Ma'am?" A soft knock preceded the turning of the knob, and in walked the woman her brother had sent.

Evelyn rose from the floor, tucking the pouch into the pocket of her dress.

"Yes?"

The woman gave a small curtsy before closing the door, the lock clicking into place. Evelyn watched as she moved to the window and pulled the drapes shut.

"What—"

The woman raised her hand, silencing Evelyn.

"I don't have much time. I must complete the reading before the elder finishes her work."

Confusion washed over Evelyn. She wasn't sure what was happening, and at the mention of an elder, she swallowed her questions. This was the work of her brother, this woman, or perhaps both. She had never indulged in the arts, only seeking out root workers when absolutely necessary. Her interest had never extended beyond a curious dabble.

The woman sank to her knees, Evelyn mirrored her movement. The woman produced a bag from the thigh pocket of her cargo pants, similar to the one Evelyn had just tucked away.

"Your brother had a reading performed," her voice low and urgent. "Your husband made a deal with the witches. Their dark magic engulfs him, this house, and soon it will take you. And the boys."

She pulled out white chalk and a large vial. Something dark red sloshed inside, making Evelyn's stomach turn.

"Do I have to drink that?" she asked, her voice barely above a whisper, but she was harshly shushed.

The woman removed the cap and stoppered it with her index finger staining the tip crimson. She brought the tinted digit to Evelyn's forehead, creating a streak down the center. She repeated the movement on herself before closing the bottle and placing the vial on the floor between them.

She sighed, rolling her shoulders.

"These witches are strong. I can feel them. Here, let me show you."

Zinhle extended her hands, palms up.

"Hands."

Evelyn quickly complied, tears seeping from her half-closed lids. She felt a pull as the lights around them flickered. Suddenly, they were somewhere else—shrouded by dilapidation. Two women stood there, the sisters. Filthy creatures, barely a step above demons.

They shifted into images of herself and Hera, and Evelyn's stomach churned as bile rose in her throat. The scenes of sex and consumption of blood played out like a horror movie. Hera riding him then herself. The sisters demands were heard even the ones whispered against the ear of Caesar's sleeping form.

Evelyn shook when the connection was severed, Zinhle lowered her hands to her thighs, a heavy silence settled in the room.

"The work has only just begun. There is still much more to be done." The woman stood, looking down at her mistress with a steely gaze.

"Shapeshifters. What more can be done? What does all of this mean? You saw and heard what they wanted." Evelyn trailed off feeling herself grow tired. The boys would never be safe.

The nurse chuckled, a sharp sound that cut through the tension.

"You pampered pack princesses, living in the palace and learning nothing of real use. You saw for yourself, madame. The American has promised the eldest of the two," she gestured toward the bed, "to those whores of the devil. He will pay for his father's power." She spoke with no malice.

She pointed at the bundle on the right, and Evelyn followed her gaze, her heart thudding violently against her breastplate.

"Please, do something. My brother—"

"Is doing all he can, ma'am. But this is something your son will have to battle when he comes of age. However," she held up her hand as Evelyn prepared to protest, "we will stand in the gap until he is ready. In the meantime, you all must leave."

The nurse inclined her head toward the babies, dropping her hand to her side.

"I have the car ready. The pilot is standing by. We will leave tonight and head back to Chad. Your brother will be waiting for us there. He will explain everything."

Evelyn's heart raced as she cast a quick glance at her twins. This was no longer about the coven or the federation. It was about her boys, and she was willing to do everything in her limited power to save them from the man she had learned to love.

"I will let you get ready. Make it quick. Your husband is unpredictable. He moves like smoke."

The woman spoke harshly and under different circumstances she would have corrected the woman's tone. But her mind was too occupied with Caesar. He wouldn't do this to them. Like herself, Caesar was always willing to toe the thin line between right and wrong. She admired the way he would casually dance with darkness but putting their children in harm's way went too far.

Evelyn grabbed a duffel bag, hurriedly tossing several items inside. She wouldn't stay—not any longer. The woman couldn't tolerate this anymore. She had to leave, and she had to take the boys with her.

Suddenly, a presence broke her concentration. She hadn't heard the door open, and as she glanced back, confusion washed over her. How had he gotten in? He wasn't even on the property; he rarely was since taking over. It was common for him to spend many nights cocooned in his office.

"Going somewhere?" Caesar emerged from the shadows, his eyes glowing with a slightly greenish hue. Evelyn nearly screamed, gripping the cashmere sweater she was holding tighter, the fabric straining under her grasp.

She froze, her heart racing as she tried to process how she missed him. The door had been locked. Her eyes lingered on it, silently hoping the mysterious woman would return. For the first time since meeting this man, she felt a deep, unsettling fear.

"She's gone. Zinhle won't bother you or us. The spy your brother sent is being picked up piece by piece from the carpet as we speak."

"She wasn't a spy. My brother sent her here to help—with the boys." She threw out the last statement, desperate to convince him.

"You sure about that? Plotting with your brother, Tulsi? Have you always been working against me?" He bared his teeth in a mocking grin as he pushed off the wall.

"Going somewhere?" silence settled between them. After nearly a minute Caesar quirked an eyebrow.

"I asked a question Evelyn. I expect an answer." His dark, glowing gaze fell on the twins swaddled in the middle of the bed, two large pillows boxing them in a soft, penetrable fortress. "You plan on taking my children away from me?"

She remained silent, part of her afraid, the other unsure if she should be truthful.

"Answer me!" he shouted, his voice echoing in the room. Evelyn jumped, dropping her sweater; he had never raised his voice at her—ever.

"I…I don't know. I don't know what's going on. You've changed." Her words came out choppy, tears brimming her eyes as she backed away, trying to create distance between them. He would close the gap; she knew it.

Caesar regarded her his mind racing wildly. Everything he had done and would do, was for them. This was about legacy. The path would be clear for the elder of his two boys. This hurt was to his core. He always thought Evelyn would never leave him.

"I'm disappointed." Caesar advanced toward her, and Evelyn instinctively stepped back, unsure of how he would react.

"I can explain," she whispered, her eyes darting back and forth like a rogue basketball. She needed a quick escape, but grabbing the twins in the process would prove nearly impossible.

"Evelyn, you're a disappointment." His gaze was watery, and his sullen demeanor made her second-guess her decision. He turned away, facing the bed.

"The children, by our law, belong to me. They are of my blood." He turned back to her. "You can leave. I give you permission to go." He reached for the doorknob, his back to her.

"You can go. Go back to your family, your father's house. But by our laws, the boys stay."

Her heart sank. She planted her feet, refusing to move.

"You know I can't leave them," Evelyn's voice was low, tinged with sadness.

"You leave me, you leave them."

Evelyn walked to the bed and sat heavily on its edge. Her gaze shifted from her husband to her reflection in the mirror. Several seconds passed before he joined her, reaching for her hand.

He interlaced his strong, muscular fingers with her slender, darkly manicured ones.

"It's me and you, Evelyn. Always."

He brought their conjoined hands up to his lips, placing a soft kiss on the back of her hand.

"Why did you do that? The boys…" she trailed off, her thoughts spiraling. Evelyn chided herself. No matter how far she traveled, she couldn't seem to escape the darkness. She was foolish to think she could leave her past. Since on American soil she had forgotten the misdeeds she committed against a friend, and how she watched as the life drained from the coal colored irises of the woman that referred to her as sister. Maybe this was Zeina's retribution.

"Evie, the boys are safe." He turned, gripping her upper arms gently but firmly.

"How? Caesar, I saw. I saw what you did. Those women, those creatures—you promised them our son." Long-suppressed panic surged within her, and Caesar felt the weight of her fear. He was losing his wife. His love. The one person he believed would stand by him through everything.

"No, no. Forget what you saw. That wasn't all of it. Those things don't know I have no intention of giving them our son. I am many things, but I wouldn't do that—not to my own flesh and blood, Evelyn. You know me better than that. Once I have all I need tomorrow night, I will go back and get rid of those filthy, vile, disgusting animals that defile and prey upon our kind." He shook her lightly.

"You believe me?" His eyes were wide, pleading.

Evelyn nodded slowly.

"Good. Enter!"

Evelyn jumped at the raised voice. A woman carrying a tray entered shakily, her gaze downward.

"Put it here." He patted the space next to Evelyn. The woman placed down the tray and left as quietly and quickly as she had come, her aged hands visibly trembling. Evelyn had never seen Mrs. Graves like this.

He released her abruptly and stood.

"I'll have the nurse come and take the boys off your hands. You're distressed, my love. You need rest—and to eat. The maids told me you aren't eating."

His demeanor shifted leaving her unsure of how to respond to the tyrant before her. The image before her a stark contrast to the man who begged for her understanding and attempted to reassure her only moments earlier.

"I would prefer to keep them here. They're already asleep." Her voice a little higher than a whisper.

"Ah, nonsense. They will be fine. If they wake, the nurse will put them back to sleep. That's what she's paid to do."

A shy nod was her only response.

Caesar nodded toward the forgotten dinner.

"Eat."

Evelyn opened and closed her mouth before her shaky voice finally reached him. "My love, I'm not—"

"Eat, Evelyn." His tone brooked no argument.

She would eat. Since the birth of the twins, Evelyn had become thinner, shrinking from a shapely size four to a two. The firmness in his voice made it clear he would not accept a refusal. She swallowed her retort. Slowly, Evelyn reached for the roll, breaking off a small piece. Carefully, she placed it between parted lips.

He nodded indicating the steak. She picked up the knife and fork, stabbing at the piece on her plate. Cutting a small portion, she repeated the steps from earlier, feeling humiliation settle over her.

Evelyn swallowed the bite of lamb followed by a few sips of water. Her stomach rolled unaccustomed to such a heavy meal. Evelyn was done and placed her hands in her lap. She would go no further; her pride had limits.

"Good. You see, my love, everyone is under my authority—including you."

He wiped away a stray tear that was tracing a path down her cheek with his thumb.

"The sooner you accept, the happier you will be."

With that, he turned and left, not bothering to close the door behind him.

15

A Bloody Ending

J ames let out a long whistle.

"Wow, this place is something, ay!" He playfully punched Winston, who had stopped at the entrance looking up. He never knew anything like this existed in Alabama.

"Hey, look—free food!" James turned, wiggling his eyebrows at Winston. "Come on." He didn't bother waiting for his comrade to follow, heading toward a young man carrying a tray of hors d'oeuvres.

Winston hissed, looking around at the few guests that had arrived early. The Coven's bourgeoisie class, he rolled his eyes as he shoved his hands deep into the trousers of the borrowed tux. Feeling smaller than when he first entered, he followed after James.

"We should head upstairs. We may be needed," Winston whispered near James's ear.

"Ah, they'll be fine." James popped another hors d'oeuvre into his mouth without a care. Winston sighed; they were part of the plan, supposed to keep watch, and when the time came for Armand to strike, he and James would take care of Caesar's guards. Winston had already rounded up the necessary enforcements.

The two made their way to the bar and stood in silence, watching.

James' excitement was palpable. Winston gave him the side eye as the young man rolled onto the balls of his feet as the well-dressed guests arrived. The hall went silent when Damien made his appearance, Hera on his arm.

"Damn, they look good." James nodded in the direction of the couple. Winston only nodded; even he had to agree. The two looked like old Hollywood stars, but his gaze lingered on Hera. She was beautiful, a wide smile warming her face. Tonight was a sharp contrast to his initial introduction to the young woman.

It was nearing the time of Caesar's arrival and Winston started to grow anxious. He just hoped this plan of Armand and Damien's worked and that he didn't lose too many of the men that had trusted him to fight. They had agreed to rebellion, and if Armand lost, they were all as good as dead.

Damien's voiced boomed, causing a second hush to fall over them.

"Welcome," Damien greeted Caesar at the entrance, his arms out-stretched. Hera stood at his side a small scowl gracing her ruby lips.

Ah brother." The hug was tight and Caesar pulled away to look down at his sister.

"Hera, good evening."

"Good evening brother," she managed a small smile, but didn't engage with him further. Damien sensing the tension guided him away into the crowd.

"Where's Evelyn? I thought she would have joined you this evening."

The American's countenance slipped, but only briefly, before his usual mask was in place.

"It's hard separating her away from the boys these days, but…" he pulled Damien further ahead, away from the crowd that was gathering around them.

"Armand. I was hoping to skip the formalities tonight. The pieces, where are they?" Excitement edged into his voice. Damien returned

Caesar's manic smile with one of his own.

"Of course. In the courtyard." Damien whispered, his arm draped over the man's shoulder.

"They all must see this," Caesar stated.

"In due time."

"No. NOW!" His voice echoed, bringing the festivities to a halt.

The musicians stopped playing, and the guests watched in fascination – others in horror. Several members of Damien's pack moved forward, ready to intervene at their alpha's command. Caesar's guards did the same, Norman moving closer than the others, ready to die for the man he swore to serve.

Damien only chuckled, "Of course, brother." The Russian broke free from Caesar and turned to face the guests.

"Everyone out to the courtyard. We have something that you all should see."

The attendees murmured excitedly among themselves as they followed the two alphas toward the large, retractable glass wall. Heavy black curtains obscured the view outside. The anticipation came over the room, weighing it down as the men pulled back the curtains and slid the wall back, exposing them to the cool breeze.

He scanned the area, expecting to see a barrel or bloody box – anything indicating his brother was no longer a problem.

"I don't see anything." Caesar was starting to grow agitated.

"Go further out and wait for it." Damien spoke, his tone nearly seductive.

Caesar did as instructed nearly reaching the middle before a figured appeared.

"Expecting to find me in pieces." Armand approached from the shadows, the gasps audible as he stepped into the light.

Hera tried to run to her brother, but was stopped by Damien.

"No, you have to let this unfold." He whispered as Hera latched onto him, wrapping her hands in the lapels of his jacket.

Caesar laughed, clutching his side.

"Is this your idea of revenge, brother? Using Damien to set this up? I didn't think you had it in you, having our sister and her intended lure me here." Caesar's hard gaze fell on Hera.

Out of nervousness, her grip tightened. So did Damien's. The gesture reassuring her that no matter how this played out, she would be safe. Damien would kill them all if any threatened her. Sensing her thoughts, Caesar's gaze shifted from her to Damien.

"He won't save you, sister. This," he gestured toward them, "is simply business. When I'm done with our brother, you're next."

"I beg to differ, Caesar. I will drop you before your brother has a chance," Damien stated, his dark green eyes reflecting the full moon.

"Until she is married she is mine! You have no rights here, Damien." Caesar positioned himself to confront the younger man.

"I am here to oversee. A blood brother has issued a challenge. As the highest-ranking member here—although I'm an outsider, I am an alpha, and I'm here to oversee the matter and ensure all parties abide by the rules," Damien stated casually, possessively wrapping an arm around Hera's waist.

"Rules? What rules? Surely, you have no right to oversee foreign coven business. This isn't a ceremony."

"Not yet." Damien flashed a smirk, playing with the corners of his full, dark pink lips.

"Per the decree Article 9, when the title of alpha is disputed within a coven, a third party recognized by the Global Lucian Council will oversee affairs until the dispute is settled," Charles announced making an appearance, Amelia at his side.

"I should have known. Father's flunky. You should have been the first to die. I should have gotten rid of you the same night as Reynolds," Caesar spat, his voice dripping with venom.

Gasps echoed around them, several guests exchanging wide-eyed glances. One of the mysteries surrounding the missing council member had finally been solved. They could easily deduce he was behind the others as well.

"Hmm, perhaps. But you've never been known for your smarts, Caesar. Yes, you should have known if you had bothered to read all 310 articles, as well as the laws handed down to us by the Lucian Council," Charles retorted, a smirk playing on his lips.

Fuming, Caesar turned to the remaining council members gathered to his right.

"What say you?" He pointed to Neil, who stood up straighter. Neil was their expert on coven law, knowing it better than the names of his numerous grandchildren.

"I'm afraid Mr. Anaheim is correct, sir. Everything is above board," Neil confirmed.

The young male DuBois hissed, white foaming spit dribbling from the down-turned corners of his mouth. He resembled a mad dog, ready to attack.

Armand watched, sensing the unnatural change overtaking his brother. Dark magic permeated the air, choking it. The ambitious blond boy he once knew was gone, replaced by this feral creature standing before him. Armand knew he would have to act decisively; the transformation had begun. He kicked off his shoes, allowing his body to deform.

Caesar laughed, his form contorting like wet paper mâché. Armand's own transformation was just as swift, eliciting more chatter from the crowd. The two circled each other, tension crackling between them.

Amelia gripped her father's arm for support. Armand was strong; her magic had merely brought forth what was already lurking deep within him, enhancing power he was unaware he possessed. It was up to him to do the rest.

The battle began; Caesar lunging first, tackling Armand to the ground. Hera swallowed a scream, quickly pursing her lips as she watched Caesar tear a chunk of flesh from Armand's left shoulder. Her older brother reciprocated, his large jaw clamping down on Caesar's back leg as the latter spun around, aiming for a second attack. The interim alpha let out a strained howl as bone crunched, the sound echoing in the ears of all the attendees and causing several of them to step back.

At one point, the pair became so entangled that it was difficult to distinguish between the brothers. As the battle raged on, howls echoed from outside, prompting many attendees to crane their necks, searching for the source of the faint noise.

Damien gave a quick but discreet nod to his servant. The short, stocky man gestured to the others, and they moved to block all entry points, preventing the curious from venturing outside.

The Russian refocused his attention on the ongoing fight, which had lost some of its intensity. The magic fueling them wasn't designed for stamina—a lesson he learned firsthand in his youth.

Caesar shifted back into human form, too weak to maintain the change. The vitriol he once displayed had dwindled, taking with it the energy he possessed at the start of the challenge. His regeneration was taking longer than anticipated; he noted that Armand's arm was healing exceptionally quickly.

Armand had pinned his brother down, his full weight pressing against Caesar's chest. Caesar followed the dark burgundy gaze to his neck, where Armand's barred fangs quivered in anticipation.

"Do it," Caesar hissed, droplets of blood coating the black tip of Armand's nose. The eldest DuBois shifted slightly, lifting some of his weight from his brother's chest.

"Do it," Caesar repeated, his voice laced with contempt.

"Show them what you're made of! For once, have some balls." His chuckle turned into a pained gurgle as he briefly turned his head to the side, spitting out blood.

"Yes, brother. I will show them what I'm made of."

Hera watched through blurred vision, unable to speak and afraid to make any noise. The sight of them destroying each other felt like the darkest day in hell, and she clung to Damien for support.

The Russian tightened his grip on his fiancée, feeling apathetic to the scene unfolding before him. If the two DuBois brothers destroyed each other, Hera would be the natural heir—and as her husband, so would he. He briefly entertained the idea of becoming the alpha of two covens, but there would be the matter of Caesar's sons to consider.

Caesar felt the dip in his bones deepen as Armand applied pressure. He lay there silently, cursing the witches. Out of the corner of his eye, he caught sight of two familiar figures—the sisters—watching with smirks on their faces.

"We will get what is ours." The faint statement echoed in his mind, the same raspy voices he had heard in the cabin.

"NO!" he screamed, turning his gaze toward the crowd.

Armand followed his line of sight to two young women standing together, watching with an unsettling intensity. Before he could comment, he felt the skin around his jaw rip as Caesar swiped at him, his arm partially transfigured and bloodied.

Armand knew this battle would never end. If he showed even a hint of mercy, his brother would continue until Armand was dead. He positioned himself, clamping with all his force around the younger's neck, piercing the jugular.

Evelyn arrived just as Caesar took his last breath. She forced her way through the crowd, standing at the edge of the battlefield. Armand shifted, bloodied fur rolling in waves. His head hung low over his brother's lifeless body. Slowly, he raised his gaze to meet Evelyn's watery eyes as she approached and knelt beside them.

"I'm sorry," was all Armand could offer. He truly regretted that it had come to this.

Evelyn swallowed a sob, thinking of her boys. They would be fatherless, but the thought was quickly interrupted. Given what Caesar had done, they would be better off. Somehow, she didn't fully believe that sentiment.

Armand scanned the crowd, searching for the two odd teens who had stood there with gleeful expressions. He had heard their whisper: 'We will get what is ours.'

Armand wanted to know what they meant, but deduced it had something to do with his brother and his new condition. He had to ask—after all, Caesar had always shared everything with his wife. He had no doubt that his brother would have confided in her about his transformation as well.

"What did my brother do?" he whispered, grasping her arms to help her stand.

She shook her head, tears spilling down her cheeks. "I don't know." A sob broke free, and she quickly covered her mouth with her hand.

"Evelyn, I think you know. Two women were here. I've never seen them before, but they said, 'We will get what is ours.' Do you know what he was mixed up in?"

Her eyes widened. The witches. They were there, which meant they could be everywhere—even at home with her boys.

"I have to go." She moved to run, but Armand wrapped his arms around her, stopping her.

"Please, tell me. What did my brother do?"

She searched his expression. He seemed genuine, and from his actions earlier, remorseful. Perhaps he could help her stop what her husband had done.

"He promised them the eldest of our sons in exchange for…" She shook her head, unsure what to call it. "This. Power."

The crowd drew closer, picking up on the conversation but not fully grasping the meaning behind the coded language. Charles felt he knew. Caesar embodied the same darkness Samuel had. The scene he witnessed eerily similar to one he had watched over thirty years ago. Even from the grave, Maximillian was paying the price with the souls of his sons.

Armand sighed. He had a duty now. The twins were his responsibility, especially since he had killed their father.

"Evelyn, no harm will come to them. I will make sure of that. You will not have to part with either of them. Do you understand?"

She wanted to believe him. Armand always held the belief that if he spoke it, the sea would part for him.

"Yes. I hope so." She gently pushed his arms away and took one last look at her husband before stepping into the crowd. They parted, allowing her to pass uninterrupted. As the wife of a slain alpha, her life was about to change.

He watched her fade into the crowd. The howls of victory from outside drew his attention. The long cry emanated from James, and Armand chuckled, closing his eyes as he glimpsed through the lens of the young man. After a week or so, the connection would be severed, and he would no longer see what James saw. Another gift that his bride-to-be had granted him.

He looked around and locked eyes with Damien. His future brother-in-law gave a curt nod and offered a small smile. Armand returned the gesture before shifting his gaze to his sister.

Her expression was pained, but it carried an understanding shared only between the two siblings. Armand wasn't sure if he would ever get over this deed, no matter how necessary it had been.

He waited silently, uncertain of what would happen next, until Charles approached.

"Congratulations, Alpha Armand." Charles gave a slight bow. "By our decree and as head of the Council, we officially recognize Armand

Nathaniel DuBois as alpha."

Applause erupted around him, with some murmuring among themselves while a few remained silent and immobile, as the impromptu celebration unfolded.

Armand searched for Amelia, and an understanding passed between them. Caesar, although his reign had been brief, had loyalists. Every alpha had his sycophants, and his brother was no different. An odd sensation rose from the pit of his stomach and settled deep within his chest. He wouldn't be able to rest; something was coming, and he could sense it, making the fine hairs on his arms stand on end.

Although the battle was won, the war had yet to come.

About the Author

Hayley M. Moon is an Alabama native with a passion for the macabre. Her debut novel, *Taming Armand*, kicks off the atmospheric *Coven Origins Series*. Her short story "Sentience" has been featured on The Word's Faire, and her work "In this Life" appears in the Hoover Library Write Club Anthology *An Unexpected Journey*. When not crafting stories, Hayley can be found doting on her cat, building her yarn collection, updating her blog The Weirdo Writes, or creating handmade coffee cup cozies. Connect with her at hayleymoon.com.

You can connect with me on:

🌐 https://hayleymoon.com

🐦 https://x.com/SimplyHayleyM

Also by Hayley M. Moon

For latest releases and events visit hayleymoon.com and follow the author to stay in the know.

 **Taming Armand: Book 1 of the Coven Origins Series**

www.ingramcontent.com/pod-product-compliance
Lightning Source LLC
Chambersburg PA
CBHW060121260626
47160CB00005B/1964